SEVEN STRANGE CLUES

"YOU SEE, IT *IS* A CLUE!"

Seven Strange Clues.   Frontispiece (Page 135)

A JUDY BOLTON MYSTERY

SEVEN STRANGE CLUES

BY

MARGARET SUTTON

Author of
THE VANISHING SHADOW
THE HAUNTED ATTIC
THE INVISIBLE CHIMES

GROSSET & DUNLAP
PUBLISHERS   NEW YORK

To Peggy and Eleanor

CONTENTS

SEVEN STRANGE CLUES

CHAPTER I

THE POSTER CONTEST

"COME on, girls! Show a little school spirit. If Farringdon Girls' High ever meant this song it's right now."

Kay Vincent had appointed herself song leader and was beating time with a ruler as she spoke. The other girls grouped on the porch of Dr. Bolton's large, rambling house joined her at the top of their voices:

"Blue and Scarlet! Blue and Scarlet!
 All join in! All join in!
 Eager for adventure; any game or contest
 Out to win!"

"That's the way we'll sing it in chapel to-morrow morning," Kay declared, "just as soon as the poster contest is announced."

"How do you know it will be announced?"

1

asked Lorraine Lee and Lois, her chum, chimed in, "Yes, Kay, how *do* you know?"

"Because I have a way of finding out things," Kay Vincent retorted. "The best drawings will be on display in Brandt's Department Store for a whole week. I guess every girl in the class is going to try for one of the prizes."

"Not every girl," Lois corrected her. "Judy isn't."

The others turned astonished eyes in the direction of Dr. Bolton's pretty, auburn haired daughter.

"For Heaven's sake, why not?" Kay wanted to know.

Judy threw back a provoking smile and swung carelessly around the porch post.

"Because I can't paint, my dear Katherine, and I hate to do anything unless I can do it well."

"But you're so clever—" Grace Dobbs insisted.

"That doesn't mean a thing, Honey. Painting pictures, like music, is a talent and if there's anything in the world that I do worse than I sing it's painting pictures."

Judy's gray eyes challenged theirs in the silence that followed.

"See? Nobody denies it. I guess you all heard me putting the rest of you off the tune when we were singing."

"Oh, no, Judy," Lois protested. "It isn't as bad as all that."

"Maybe not. But it's pretty awful. If they were offering a booby prize I might try for that. But what could I paint? It's for Health Week, I suppose, and we are expected to make something that's good for us. I might draw an egg, but even then there would be lights and shadows to put in."

The others laughed at this, all except Grace Dobbs. She was known to her friends and family as "Honey" and had not always been a member of this select group of high school girls. Judy had solved the mystery of her real name and helped restore her to her own family. Now she seemed as much a part of the group as though she had lived in Farringdon all her life.

"Please don't disappoint us, Judy," she begged. "You are the one who inspires the rest of us. If you back out the whole contest will fall flat. I never did any kind of art work before but I do want to try for this prize and if I thought only those who were good at drawing were going to enter pictures I would never dare enter mine.''

"There will be plenty of bad pictures," Kay Vincent assured her. But Kay spoke with a lift of her chin and she might as well have added, ''but mine won't be one of them.''

Judy could see that the problem was a real one to Honey. She was still new to their ways of doing things and often timid about entering into their good times. It was her quiet, unobtrusive manner as well as her thoughtfulness of others that had endeared her to the group. No name, they all declared, except "Honey" could quite describe this welcome newcomer. Now Judy wanted to help and the thought came to her that she could.

"I think I will try for the prize after all," she announced, "and I have the grandest idea, Honey. Something that will be sure to help both of us.''

"Do tell me," Grace Dobbs coaxed. "If it's like most of your ideas I'm sure we all want to hear it.''

But before Judy had a chance to divulge her idea she was interrupted by an animated girl who rushed up on the porch waving a white sheet of paper. It was Irene Lang, one of the silk mill workers whom Judy had befriended. Of necessity, she went to a different high school where classes were held in the evening.

"Judy!" she called out. "Do tell me what you think of this. It's all ready to paint."

"Your poster!" she exclaimed. "Irene! How fast you work! Why, we just heard about the contest this minute and here your poster is all started!"

Taking it in her hand, Judy studied the drawing and the carefully printed wording, DRINK A QUART OF MILK DAILY. The picture was of a child standing beside a table. On the table stood a half filled milk bottle and the child was drinking from a glass. She held it up for the other girls to see.

"Lovely!" Lorraine Lee exclaimed. "When did you hear about the contest?"

"They announced it to the evening classes last Friday," Irene replied. "You see, we do need extra time because we all work during the day. But you seem to have been told too."

"Kay just told us," Honey put in. "It wasn't announced in school."

"Oh, then you must know some of the mill girls," Irene said, turning to Kay.

The Vincent girl drew herself to her full height. "Indeed! You are quite mistaken. I never associate with any of the mill girls."

A little sound of protest escaped Judy's lips. She liked Irene too well to let Kay hurt her. She started to say something unkind but before she could think of anything Lois had cleverly changed the subject and they were talking about the poster again.

"How did you do that adorable face? You're always surprising us, Irene. First it was your violin playing at Judy's Halloween party. We couldn't guess who it was until you took your mask off. Then your singing. But who ever thought you had a talent for drawing too? How Heaven has blessed you!"

"Has it?" Irene's lips curved into a queer, crooked smile. "Sometimes I wonder. I have always wanted to draw but not as much as I want to play and sing. Garry draws though and he helped me a little this noon. Of course he didn't do any of it," she explained quickly in answer to Kay Vincent's critical look, "just gave me a few pointers about perspective and things like that. He's awfully nice, isn't he, Judy?"

"Stephen Garry? Why yes, I liked him. He and another boy just rented half of our garage," she explained to the others. "They board at Irene's house."

"Oh!" Kay lifted a disdainful eyebrow. "You take in boarders and work in the silk mill too? Irene Lang, I don't see how you stand it."

"One learns to stand a lot of things," Irene returned, concealing her hurt feelings with her usual cheerful smile. "Besides, the boarders are no trouble and they're company for Dad. The other one, Lon Edwards, sat all morning playing chess with him. Poor Dad can hardly move from his chair. Judy's father was over this morning and he thinks it's some kind of poisoning from the paint they used in the factory where he used to work."

"Dad told me," Judy said, giving her friend's hand a sympathetic squeeze. "I know it's hard for you and you're a brick to keep up with school and music. And now this poster.

Any other girl would be too dead-tired to even attempt it. Tell me, Irene, have you bought your paints?''

''I—I couldn't afford—'' Irene began.

''Good!'' exclaimed Judy. ''Then you can borrow mine. Not only that,'' she added mysteriously, ''you can borrow my work-bench too. It's really being built for my brother but we girls can have the use of it. I was just about to tell Honey when you came along.''

''A work-bench! So that's what your big idea was! And you really mean that Irene and I can come here to do our posters?'' Grace Dobbs asked.

''Yes, Honey.'' Judy smiled at her pleasure. ''Irene's boarders have promised to build the bench for me out of some old planks that were stored in the garage. I thought of an ideal place for it and you could never guess where.''

''Not the attic!'' The girls' voices were lowered. All of them had heard of the many mysterious things Judy and her brother had discovered there. The ghosts were ''brought to light'' at her never-to-be-forgotten Halloween party.

"Just the opposite," Judy laughed, "the cellar!"

Irene and Honey exchanged glances. The poster contest promised adventure, the kind of shivery adventure that Judy delighted in. Both of them were anxious to share it.

CHAPTER II

SOMEONE WHISTLING

"I'M SORRY about Kay," Judy told Irene after the others were gone. "It's just the way she is. I wouldn't have anything to do with her only she's always tagging around with Lois and Lorraine because she thinks they're 'society.' You know the rest of us don't feel at all the way she does."

"I know you and Honey don't," Irene replied. "And it's awfully good of you to let us work in your cellar. Only—only aren't you afraid it will be too dark down there?"

"It's well lighted. And we're going to build the bench right under the window. Perhaps you've never seen the cellar."

Irene admitted that she hadn't. But she had heard so many queer things about the house that she felt, quite naturally, a little timid about entering the darkest part of it. The cellar might be haunted too.

10

"Vine Thompson's spirit, I suppose!"

It was like Judy to laugh away her fears. Rumors of ghosts had not prevented the Bolton family from moving in and transforming "the haunted house" into a comfortable home. It had belonged to Harry Vincent, Kay's father. He had purchased it along with all the houses in the row above it, intending to rent it to the new foreman at the furniture factory. That was just about the time he gave up the job himself and began making money through other channels. The new foreman, however, objected to the high rental. But Harry Vincent had no difficulty in renting the house, shortly afterwards, to Vine Thompson, a woman who bought and sold stolen goods. Both of her sons were robbers and it was through Judy's efforts that the younger one was apprehended. The woman herself was murdered and, for that reason, Harry Vincent found it impossible to dispose of the house where the crime had been committed.

Of course he wouldn't live in it himself. Although it was a well-appointed house with all modern conveniences and spacious grounds it was too close to the "poor section" to suit his family's newly cultivated taste for high society.

Quite the contrary was true of Dr. Bolton. He found it convenient to live just on the dividing line where Grove Street ended and Upper Grove Street began. Below the dividing line were the pretentious homes of Farringdon's substantial citizens. Above it the mill workers lived in shabby little houses. But the kindhearted doctor numbered his patients among rich and poor alike and his daughter, although considered one of the select "down town" crowd, had broken through the invisible barrier and succeeded in making friends among the mill workers too.

The ghosts in the house were partly respon sible for that. The superstitious neighbors in the row had been firm believers in them and no one had been more surprised than Irene Lang when the mystery was finally solved.

Judy's desire to get to the bottom of things persisted. Even her brother, Horace, who had once been timid, found a peculiar joy in tracking down mysteries. He was a reporter for the Farringdon *Daily Herald* and his sister's flare for "detecting" had gained for him many choice bits of news.

At dinner table that evening Judy had a great many interesting things to tell her family. She went into detail about the poster contest and set them all wondering where Kay Vincent got her advance information. Horace, who had been away from home all day, knew nothing of the two men who had rented the garage.

"What are we going to do with the lumber that's stored there?" he asked after Judy had told him.

"They thought we could put it in the cellar. They were very nice about it and even offered to help build something with the lumber. I suggested a work-bench." Judy cast a sidelong glance at her brother. "Would you like that?"

"Would I!" the boy exclaimed. "Gee! What fellow wouldn't? But what gets me, Judy, is how on earth you happened to think of it."

"The usual selfish motive," she replied. "I want one end of it for my paints. Honey hasn't any room to work in the apartment and Irene can't afford to buy paints so I told them both they could work here and use mine.''

''And that, Son,'' Dr. Bolton finished for her, ''is 'the usual selfish motive.' ''

''But Dad,'' Judy protested, not quite understanding. ''Irene draws beautifully. She has her poster all ready and I'm sure she won't waste the paints. Imagine what it would be like being able to sing and draw too. Goodness! I wish I had a talent.''

''You have,'' the doctor answered quietly. ''A very rare talent, Judy girl.''

Later, when she was in bed, Judy remembered her father's words and wondered about them. Surely he couldn't believe she had a talent for art. But what else could he have meant? Judy thought over the events of the day and found herself actually looking forward to starting that poster. There was plenty of room in the cellar and plenty of light——

Something had made her think of light. What, she asked herself, could cause that queer glow across the garage driveway. She could see it through her bedroom window. Throwing a robe over her shoulders, she tiptoed across the room and looked out.

The light on the gravel driveway made the

pebbles look ghostly white and an unreasonable
fear took possession of Judy before she realized that it was only the electricity that had
been left on in the cellar.

"I wonder who was the last one down
there," she mused. "Whoever it was, I suppose it's up to me to go down and turn out the
light."

Just inside the door at the head of the cellar
stairs she stumbled over Blackberry, the kitten
that Peter Dobbs had given her. Peter was
Honey's brother and Judy had known him since
they were children together in the little town of
Roulsville.

"What a forgetful person I am," she chided
herself. "Why, I felt perfectly sure I put
Blackberry outside before I went to bed."

With the kitten in her arms, she reached for
the button to turn off the light. Her hand
paused midway. Someone down cellar was
whistling!

"Horace!" she called softly. "Are you
there?"

No answer.

"Dad!" This time her voice was louder
"Is that you?"

Still no answer. But the whistling ceased. It hadn't sounded like Horace or her father either, but who else could it be? Judy decided to go down herself and investigate.

CHAPTER III

BREAKING GLASS

THE cellar stairs were steep and Judy's floppy slippers almost made her stumble. Half way down she stopped and stood clutching the kitten. There really might be something mysterious in the cellar and she wanted to be the one to discover it. But if it whistled. . . . She shuddered. Lately she had been listening to detective stories on the radio and always, before a crime was about to be committed, there came that ghostly whistling. It might be some kind of a warning.

"Goose!" she said to herself and resolved to quit thinking such things. The sensible procedure would be to go on down and make sure that the back cellar door was locked. That would be the first entrance a burglar would look for. Then the windows. Judy reached up and gave the one near the stairs an experimental push. Yes, it was bolted securely on

17

both sides. Then she tried the other windows and the door. All of them were locked from the inside.

"It must have been my imagination," she said aloud. "Or was it you, Blackberry, whistling through your whiskers?"

Her father called down from upstairs. "What's the matter, Judy girl? Was it the door bell?"

"Oh, no! The door bell didn't ring."

"But I thought I heard you talking to some-one," the doctor insisted.

"It was only Blackberry," Judy called back, feeling a little foolish. "Someone shut him down cellar and forgot to turn off the light."

Irene's boarders came early in the morning to help move the lumber. Judy observed them more closely this time and thought how young they were. She left her breakfast to watch them work.

"Good morning, Miss Bolton," Stephen Garry called out in a friendly voice. "Thanks for telling us about that boarding place. It's a dandy."

"I'm glad you like it," she replied, coming closer to watch. "Irene is a friend of mine.

She's a clever girl and very much interested in music.''

"I took it she was interested in art," he said. "Some contest or other down at the department store and she's trying for the prize."

"Oh, yes, she was telling me." Judy forgot that the young men were almost strangers in her interest in Irene and the poster she was painting. "I'm trying for the prize too," she went on. "At first I didn't intend to but last night Dad said something about talent and if I have any I want the world to know it."

"That's the spirit!" exclaimed Lon Edwards. He was the older of the two and seemed a likeable fellow although, in some indefinable way, different from most of the boys that Judy knew.

"It was awfully good of you to help us," she told them after they were finished with their work. "I suppose you will be moving your car in right away."

"Yes, Miss Bolton, right away. It's a dandy new one," Stephen Garry told her. "Some day I hope you'll consent to ride in it!"

"I'd like to," she replied, trying to be polite, "but this poster contest will take most of my spare time. I'm in high school, you see, and have stacks of homework.''

She wondered why Lon Edwards chose just that moment to nudge his companion and give him a black look which, apparently, meant something. Her excuse seemed to satisfy Stephen Garry, however, as no more was said about riding in the car. The next day the two men drove it into the garage.

It was a long, maroon-colored car, the only unusual thing about it being the fact that the shades on the rear windows were closely drawn. Judy suspected the men of carrying carpenter's tools on the back seat during the day. At any rate they had done a good job piling the lumber into the cellar. Judy went down there with her brother to help decide upon a suitable place for the new work-bench. She told Horace about Garry's invitation and Lon Edwards' significant nudge.

''Don't go, Sis,'' he warned her. ''Stick to the old crowd. They're safe. I never trust these young fellows who drive around in expensive cars——''

''Arthur does,'' she interrupted.

Arthur was Lois' tall, distinguished-looking

brother and a successful young engineer. He and Peter Dobbs as well as Judy's brother shared in most of the girls' adventures.

"Arthur is a Farringdon-Pett," Horace reminded her. "I never heard of any Garrys who were substantial citizens of Farringdon."

"The car had Canadian license plates," Judy remembered. "Who knows but they may be substantial citizens of Quebec? Anyway they know how to get what they want even if they do have to work for it." She was thinking of the morning when they first came to the house inquiring for rooms. When Mrs. Bolton recommended Irene's place they still insisted that they wanted garage space and finally persuaded her to let them move the lumber.

"But they don't get my little sister. See?" Horace pulled one of her auburn ringlets to give the statement emphasis. Then started toward the stairs on a run.

"You're forgetting something," Judy called after him. "You're forgetting to bolt the cellar door."

"So I am!" he exclaimed, turning suddenly on his heel. "I suppose it's even more important now that we have tenants in the garage

—What the Heck!'' He interrupted himself with this exclamation as his body was thrown, suddenly, in mid-air.

Judy couldn't keep from laughing. "The planks that our obliging tenants piled in the cellar. I'm afraid they are going to be dreadfully in the way."

"I'm not afraid so. I know so."

Horace sat down on the end of one of them to rub his bruised ankle. His sister, who had perched herself on the other end of the plank, got up suddenly.

"What was that?" she cried.

Horace glared at her. "That, my dear, was your brother taking an awful licking, thanks to you!"

"Oh, I'm sorry. I didn't mean to let you bump—" She broke off suddenly. "There! I heard it again!"

"Heard what?"

"Something. I don't know what. But it sounded like breaking glass—right here in the cellar."

"It's a wonder it wasn't breaking bones," Horace answered dryly. He was still rubbing his bruised ankle but Judy paid no attention.

"Maybe you had something breakable in your pockets when you fell," she suggested hopefully.

He felt to see. "Nope. Nothing in this one . . . or this. Gosh! Judy, what do you suppose it was?"

"I wish I knew. Maybe something on the furnace. There's that little glass thing. . . . But that's all right. Not even cracked."

They had been examining the water level gauge while she talked. Now they opened the furnace door to see if anything out of the ordinary could have been thrown into the fire. Days were getting warmer and it had been banked all day but a small tongue of blue flame showed them nothing unusual within.

"And it couldn't have been upstairs," Judy added, "because it didn't *sound* upstairs."

Horace had been thinking. Any one could tell when Horace thought because he always ran his fingers through his hair. It made him look a little wild. Now he was scowling at the pile of boards.

"Judy, we've got to get rid of these blamed things," he said.

"Just because you fell over them?"

"No, that isn't the reason," he declared. "There may be something *under* them."

"You really think so?" Judy cried excitedly. "Then let's get the boys to work on that bench right away and find out what it is."

CHAPTER IV

SO THIS IS ART!

STEPHEN GARRY'S car was just leaving the garage and the shades were still down. Lon Edwards had stayed behind to close the doors but when Judy called out to him about building the bench he promptly opened them again and drove the car back inside.

"Sure," he agreed. "Be glad to do it. To-day's as good as any other day. We've got hammer, nails and saw all ready to go to work."

Judy smiled knowingly at Horace who was just emerging from the cellar. "I told you they probably kept tools behind those fancy curtains."

He nodded and grinned. Then he showed the two young men the place that they had decided upon for the bench. It was to be right under the back cellar window where the sunshine poured in all afternoon. A convenient electric light was right overhead so that any one could work either by day or night.

They proved to be efficient carpenters. By evening the pile of planks had been transformed into an attractive and substantial bench. But not a sign of any broken glass had been found underneath them. Judy went down cellar to watch again as soon as school was out and found Stephen Garry just finishing. The top of the bench he planed almost as smooth as a drawing board and underneath were two long drawers, one for Horace and one for Judy. He offered to buy Judy's show card colors on his way downtown to the hardware store. The drawer pulls were still to be attached.

"You're too kind," Judy told him. "We shouldn't let you do all this work without pay."

"That's nothing to what I would do," he replied, giving Judy a curious look that she was at a loss to interpret.

Later when she showed the bench to Peter Dobbs there was no mystery about his feelings.

"Gosh! Judy," he exclaimed. "I could have done as good a job as that. I could have bought the show card colors too. I did buy a few for Honey and she has them with her."

"I thought maybe we might work at the new bench tonight," she ventured.

"I wish we could," Judy replied, "but Arthur has invited me to a concert and I couldn't disappoint him. You don't mind working alone?"

"Oh, no," Honey assured her. "You two run along and have a good time. Peter will stay down here with me."

"Sorry, Honey, but I can't," her brother replied. "Got to study law tonight and the books are back at the apartment. But I'll be here to take you home."

In her mind Judy could hear that uncanny whistling, then the strange sound of breaking glass. Feeling a little guilty about leaving her friend alone in the cellar, she surprised her with a sudden kiss.

" 'By, Honey—and good luck with your poster."

The concert itself was not up to Judy's expectations. All the élite of Farringdon were there dressed in formal attire. But most of them, she observed, looked a little bored. So, instead of sitting primly in her seat she kept turning her head to see who else was there. Kay Vincent, of course, in a box seat where everyone could see her dazzling new gown. Her father, the leading party's candidate for Mayor, sat beside her. Judy also recognized Chief of Police Kelly, and smiled at him. But what surprised her was the fact that Irene's boarders were there. Usually people from the factory section did not attend concerts in the Farringdon Academy of Music.

After the concert Stephen Garry waited to speak to Judy. He was introduced to Arthur and his sister who had come with Donald Carter, another reporter from the *Daily Herald* and Horace's rival for front page news. Afterwards Judy told them about Irene's boarders building a work-bench in the cellar. "And I expect Grace Dobbs is busy painting her poster this minute," she continued. "I promised to lend it to Irene tomorrow—the bench and my paints too. So if you want any extra colors, Lois, you'll know where to find them."

"Thanks, Judy," she replied, "but Lorraine and I have borrowed Mother's sewing room for the purpose. She doesn't use it much any more as good dressmakers are hard to find and we like to buy our things in the shops. But if *you* run short of colors you might come to me."

"That's more likely," Arthur agreed, "with

so many others using them. Have you decided on your subject?''

''Fruit,'' Judy replied shortly, ''because it's easy.''

That was her thought the next day when she bought oranges, bananas and a shiny apple at a fruit stand. Anybody ought to be able to copy such simple objects and EAT FRUIT FOR HEALTH was a good slogan for her poster.

Just outside the store she met Grace Dobbs.

''You went home early last night, didn't you?'' Judy asked. ''Was there a reason?''

Honey seemed surprised. ''Why no, I went home quite late. It was nearly eleven and I felt a little tired. Painting takes a lot out of any one. And I'm not very sure of myself. How did you enjoy the concert?''

''Fair,'' she replied, ''as concerts go. I'm afraid I don't appreciate classical music. How did you make out with your poster?''

''I'm not sure. I'll do a little touching up with my own paints and come again tomorrow night if I may.''

''You may.'' Judy hesitated. ''Honey, did you—did you *hear* anything while you were in the cellar?''

Suspense! And then came Honey's answer. "No, not a thing."

She explained that she had waited merely because the question surprised her and at first she thought Judy was joking.

"Why," she asked, "did you?"

"It wasn't anything *much*," the doctor's daughter replied. "It's just that living in Vine Thompson's house has made me suspicious of little noises. Sometimes I wish she had been murdered somewhere else."

"Judy!" Honey gasped. "You never told me she was murdered!"

"I thought you knew," she answered. "Why, everyone else in school knows it and certainly Kay Vincent talks enough about it. She never will get over her father's generosity in letting us move in. She forgets the fact that we bought and paid for the house after nobody thought it was haunted any more. You knew that the mill girls said Vine Thompson's spirit walked around crying for revenge—and they believed it too. Even Irene believed it. But after I gave that big party here everybody seemed to think the ghosts had disappeared. I thought so too. . . . But I shouldn't talk this way.

I'll be frightening you and you won't want to come back and finish your poster."

"Of course I will." Honey laughed and caught Judy's hand in her own. "You don't know me *yet*, Judy Bolton. Why, I like exciting things every bit as much as Peter does and you know what a nose he has for adventure."

"Do I?" she exclaimed. "We'll look for both of you tomorrow night. Now I must run home and begin my own poster." She displayed the open bag of fruit. "This is to be the subject."

A blue bowl was found in the kitchen closet and as soon as her homework was done Judy began arranging the fruit ready to copy. At first she put it all in the dish. Then she decided that the bananas looked better hanging over one edge. She eyed the arrangement critically and began copying before the sun was gone from the cellar window. It made the oranges looke brilliant and, the drawing finished quickly, Judy was soon ready to paint her fruit. She mixed her brightest color and began.

All at once the sunlight disappeared and Judy was obliged to turn on the electricity. She pressed the button and listened, half expecting to hear the whistling sound. It *might* have had something to do with the current.

"No," she decided, "it wasn't that."

The artificial light on the work-bench gave the oranges Judy was copying an altogether different appearance. She added a touch of red and tried to shade them. The rough-appearing surface seemed most difficult and, after several unsuccessful attempts, she gave up trying and began on the bananas. They were easier. A little color from the blue bowl ran into them but Judy thought it didn't matter. Anyone might think the bananas weren't quite ripe.

"Working hard?" Horace greeted her from the head of the cellar stairs. He was home from the newspaper office and Judy realized that it must be dinner time. He came closer to see her picture.

"Golly! It's bright," he exclaimed. "What is it? The sun?"

"Of course not, Silly. Can't you see it's in a blue dish?"

"Oh, pardon! Pardon!" Horace made a low bow. "I thought that was the sky."

"You had the picture upside down."

"So I did. Hmm! I see now. It's an orange. Looks as if it's beginning to go bad. But Judy, seriously, orange leaves aren't yellow and they aren't as long as this."

He pointed to the daub of yellow paint that was supposed to represent a banana.

Ordinarily Judy would have laughed at his mistake. But she had really tried her best and if the picture was as bad as all that her time had simply been wasted.

"Oh, what's the use!" she cried, almost in tears. "I might as well tear it up and be done with it."

"Ah, I wouldn't do that," Horace objected. "Now if you'd just put a bit more green in those leaves——"

"But they're *not* leaves. They're bananas. Can't you see the dish of fruit I'm copying?"

Horace bit his lip. Judy could see that he was trying not to laugh and it angered her. "Well, if you're so smart, I might as well tell you why I'm doing this. Honey didn't want to go into the contest because she thought her drawing would be the poorest in the class. So I went in on purpose to make a worse one!"

"If that's the case," her brother replied,

"you're doing beautifully. But even Charity takes vacations and I wouldn't be surprised if Mother has something upstairs a bit more appetizing than your painted fruit. C'mon, Judy."

"I'm coming."

She pushed the brushes into a pile, covered the bottles of paint and then turned the drawing on its face so that if Irene came in again she would not see it.

CHAPTER V

Judy's caller that evening was not Irene Lang. Peter Dobbs and his sister came instead.

"I didn't do any more of this," Honey explained exhibiting the square envelope that she carried to protect her poster. "Just couldn't get going and I thought maybe your cellar would be an inspiration."

"It wasn't to me."

Judy told them what a botch she had made of her own poster.

"No one has seen it but Horace," she went on, "and I hope no one does. If you find a piece of paper flat on its face please leave it that way. I'm disgusted with it."

Peter grinned. "That being the case you would probably welcome a vacation from painting. We might take in a movie and leave Honey to work alone. How about it?"

Again Judy thought of the cellar and its

35

possible perils, but she had heard nothing unusual that afternoon and had about decided
that the whistling noise must have been the
wind. The breaking glass was more of a puzzle but, on the whole, nothing to worry about.
Not as much, she thought ruefully, as that
dreadful painting. She didn't want to work
with Honey or Irene either. Perhaps they
would ask embarrassing questions too and mistake her oranges for suns and her bananas for
green leaves.

When Peter told her that there was a double feature at the Rialto Judy found it easy
to make up her mind. Promising to be home
early, she and the young law student started
at once.

Peter's cheerfulness was contagious. Afterwards Judy confessed that she enjoyed the
movie more than the concert that she attended
with Arthur. Not knowing how well both of
these boys liked her she could not know the
satisfaction it gave Peter to hear her say that.
She did know that they spent more time over
their sodas than they intended to spend. The
hands on the court house clock pointed to midnight when they passed the public square.

"Goodness!" she exclaimed. "Imagine Honey in the cellar all this time!"

The very thought of it made Judy shiver.

When they came in sight of the house Peter pointed out a light in the cellar window. "Still at it," he commented. "Most likely she had an inspiration and paid no more attention to the time than we did."

"Just the same," Judy replied, forgetting caution. "I would rather not be in that cellar at midnight. There's something spooky about it."

They hurried into the house and called out to Honey, telling her it was after midnight. Almost immediately the girl, rather white and shaky, Judy thought, came running out of the cellar.

"We must hurry!" she exclaimed as Peter took the square envelope to carry for her. "Grandma will be worrying."

"Did you do much painting?" Judy ventured just as they were ready to leave.

"I'm through with it," Honey called back over her shoulder. "Goodnight, Judy."

Peter added his "Goodnight" and they were gone.

"Something has happened," Judy said to herself. She wondered just what Honey meant when she said she was through with her poster. Had she finished the painting or given up working on it for some unknown reason? But Judy's curiosity was not great enough to cause her to go into the cellar again until morning. Then Horace was there ahead of her.

"I must say you and Honey have made a dreadful mess of this place," he called up in an irritated tone.

Judy was busy helping in the dining room. She hadn't slept well and was feeling cross.

"What's the matter with it?" she snapped back.

"Everything's the matter with it. Come down and see for yourself."

Remembering Honey's haste the night before, Judy went down half expecting to see the work of robbers or something equally frightening. Instead, the work-bench was almost as she, herself, had left it. Brushes were unwashed. Paint bottles were uncovered and papers were scattered carelessly about. But that was all. No evidence of anything except Honey's haste and Judy had been sure of that the previous night. At any rate, Horace didn't need to be so fussy about it. She told him so.

"It isn't fussy," he declared, "to like things in order. If any part of this work-bench is mine I want it kept in decent shape."

"Straighten it yourself then," Judy retorted. She had dressed herself for Sunday dinner and had no desire to soil her clothes cleaning the cellar, especially when the family expected to go out in the car that afternoon.

In school the next day Judy learned a little more about shading colors, among other things the use of white paint in bringing out lights and shadows. The blue bowl might be improved by a streak of white light here and there. The bananas, too, she might cover with white and then put in the yellow as it should be. It would be easier to do over the whole poster but each student was given one, and only one, sheet of paper on which to paint. These sheets were furnished by the department store and at the top had dotted lines for the contestant's name, class, age and home address. If they were lost or spoiled no more sheets were available.

"That's the trouble," Judy said to herself and heaved a sigh that came clear up from her toes. "If I only could have started the thing right. Why did I draw it in such a hurry?"

One consolation was the fact that the apple and other oranges were still to be colored. After Judy had her new bottle of white paint she started home eager, once more, to work on her poster.

It did make her feel just a little ashamed when she saw how Horace had tidied up the cellar. He had washed the brushes and had them all drying in a neat row on an old tooth brush holder. That, also, was washed and everything else was dusted and in order. Only Judy's poster was left exactly where she put it, on its face. She turned it over and a dismayed cry escaped her lips. Some of the yellow paint had smeared!

"You should have known better than to turn it over when it was still wet," Horace scolded her.

He came into the cellar just as his sister made the discovery. Even her white paint could not cover up all the smudges. Yellow was smeared across the blue bowl making it look almost as green as the bananas.

"You might name it A STUDY IN GREEN," he suggested whimsically.

. "Paris green," Judy said and her voice sounded almost mournful. "Oh, why did I ever enter this contest? My better judgment told me all along that it was no use."

Horace grinned.

"You entered the contest to make a worse drawing than Honey's," he reminded her.

He perched himself on one of the tall stools beside the bench and sat there watching his sister. She held the drawing in her hand for fully a minute, studying it. Then she turned on him.

"Well, smarty, maybe it won't be worse than Honey's. From what she said Saturday night she seems pretty discouraged, too."

"What did she say?" Horace asked.

" 'I'm through with it.' That's exactly what she said. And I'm not through," Judy added vigorously. "At least I can make a good apple. We copied one in drawing class today and learned all about lights and shadows. I hurried right home to do it before I forgot and now, my dear brother, if you'll excuse me, I shall proceed.''

"Certainly, my *dear* sister. Allow me to present—your fruit.'' With exaggerated courtesy, he placed the bowl beside the window where she could see better to copy it. "Mind if I watch?'' he asked.

"Not at all.'' Judy was busy mixing a mellow shade of red paint and had not looked up. She took one of the brushes from the holder and dipped it. Then she glanced at the fruit dish ready to copy the rosy cheeked apple.

"Horace!'' she cried. "Put that back.''

He stared at her.

"Put it back, I said.'' She repeated this in a hurt and angry voice. "I think you're mean, Horace Bolton. *Please* put it back.''

"Put what back? Good grief! I haven't taken anything.''

"You have, too. You've taken my apple.'' This time she stared at him.

"Your apple? Why Judy, I haven't seen any apple. Where was it? Not in the fruit dish?''

"You must know it was.''

"But I didn't see it,'' he insisted. "Gee,

Sis, I wouldn't do anything to spoil your poster. You ought to know that.''

Her eyes narrowed. Just how sincere was
he? Judy remembered seeing the apple Sunday morning when he cleaned the cellar and
if nobody had been down there since, he must
have taken it.

''And if you're still teasing,'' she warned
him, ''you're carrying it a little too far. You
wait here and I'll find out from Mother just
what's been happening.''

In a few minutes Judy returned. Her lips
straightened into a hard line as she faced her
brother.

''Mother says you're to give up that apple.
And do it right away,'' she commanded. ''You
have no right to make me spoil my poster.''

''I haven't any apple—'' he began but she
interrupted furiously.

''Nobody's been in this cellar since yesterday morning. The furnace is out and so nobody came down here to shovel coal. There
weren't any men to read gas and electric meters
either because Mother said so. You're just
playing a trick to make fun of me and I think
you're mean—mean——''

"It would be a mean trick, but I didn't do it." His voice sounded convincing and Judy had to listen. "You've got to believe me, Sis. I did *not* take that apple."

"Well then, who did?"

"That's what I propose to find out," he declared and started toward the back cellar door.

CHAPTER VI

THE MISSING STACK OF PAPERS

Standing with her back against the work-bench, Judy watched her brother try first the door and then the windows. All of them were bolted—had been bolted ever since Sunday morning. Since the furnace was out for the summer there could be no reason for entering the cellar except to get at the work-bench or the fruit that stood in the window behind it.

"What do you make of it?" Horace asked. He had abandoned his search for unlocked entrances and stood beside Judy looking puzzled.

"I still think you're to blame," his sister replied. "If you didn't take the apple on purpose then you probably knocked it off by accident when you moved the dish."

"Say!" he exclaimed. "I hadn't thought of that. Let's hunt for it."

Accordingly, they both knelt on the floor and searched in the scattered gravel under the work-bench. But it was Judy who found what she considered conclusive evidence of her brother's guilt. She held up her find for him to see.

It was an apple core.

"Somebody's eaten the apple!" he exclaimed.

"That's apparent." Judy's voice was like ice. "And I suppose you're going to try to tell me that you don't know who that somebody was."

"I certainly don't know."

"Well, I don't know either," she confessed, "but I am sure of this much. There aren't many burglars who would enter a house for the sake of eating an apple and even burglars can't get in through locked doors and windows. You can't blame ghosts either, even if we were silly enough to believe in them. Ghosts wouldn't eat. But boys would and I know one boy in particular who is very fond of apples."

"I may be fond of them, Judy, but I knew you had the fruit all arranged——"

"And you made fun of it."

"Even so, I wouldn't lie about what I did. You know that. I cleaned up here but I didn't touch that fruit. I did pile up a stack of papers to burn though and before they're disposed of you might look them over. I don't want to spoil anything for you. And Sis?"

"Yes?"

"I'm darned sorry about that poster."

Judy studied his face, trying to make up her mind what to say but the door bell ringing upstairs interrupted her thoughts. When she saw it was Grace Dobbs she decided to ask her advice before she forgave Horace.

"Come up to my room, Honey," she said. "I've been waiting to talk to you for ages."

"About something important?"

"Sort of. Are you in a hurry?"

Honey smiled. "Sort of. But I'll listen." She led the way upstairs and seated herself on the edge of Judy's bed. "Now ask me anything. I'll tell the truth, the whole truth and nothing but the truth, so help me——"

"Please be serious," Judy interrupted. "I've been teased and teased until I almost hate people for it. Just now an apple disappeared out of my fruit dish and Horace declares he didn't take it. Nobody has been in the cellar since he was and so I don't know whether to believe him or not. Would you?"

"I think I would. What was he teasing you about?"

"My poster," Judy replied. "Honey, it's awful. I'll never dare enter it. I turned it over before it was quite dry and it's smeared with yellow paint. Horace thinks I'm dreadfully careless and he even fussed at me because you left the work-bench in a mess. What happened?"

"Nothing." Honey rose and began adjusting her hat. "Nothing happened at all. I guess I am careless and I'm sorry if I made extra work for you."

"You didn't," Judy put in quickly. "Horace is the one who cleaned up. He covered the paints, washed the brushes and piled the scattered papers beside the furnace all ready to burn."

"How nice of him!" Honey exclaimed. "If you'll excuse me now, Judy, I think I'll run along and offer my apologies to him on the way out. Or is he down cellar?"

"He was. Must you go, Honey?"

"Homework, my dear," and she hurried out of the room.

Judy could hear her footsteps going down the stairs. What would she say to Horace, Judy wondered. This business of apologizing was not much to her liking, especially since she was not sure. . . . That was just it. How difficult sometimes to be sure of things. And who besides Horace could have eaten that apple?

"Your brother must have gone out," Honey called up. "He wasn't in the cellar. Tell him I'm sorry about the work-bench, will you, Judy?"

Promising that made matters even worse. Just the same Judy promised, all the time dreading it. Apologizing for someone else was almost as bad as apologizing for herself and the more she thought of it the more certain Judy felt that Horace had started out to tease, found that he was carrying it too far and tried to crawl out of it. It wasn't like her brother, to be sure, but of all the characters Judy knew, his was the most changeable. Once he had been so timid that other reporters called him "Sister" but now he was always on hand whenever word came of hold-ups, burglaries or even murders. A fascinating business, Judy thought, but not one which encouraged truth telling.

"I might as well face facts," she said aloud,

facing herself in her long mirror as she said it. "People just will crawl out of things and of course Horace would be ashamed of eating that apple. I'll apologize for Honey because she asked me to, but I'll not apologize for myself until I'm sure he isn't to blame."

That decided, she brought out her school books and proceeded to do her lessons. She had saved some old test papers that had been handed back because they might come in handy for reviewing. Sometimes the same questions were asked over again in class. But where were the test papers? Then Judy remembered the papers that Horace had piled beside the furnace and went down cellar to search among them. Blackberry, who still cherished hopes of finding mice in the house, followed her.

The white gravel on the cellar floor annoyed Judy whenever she went down there alone. It made such a queer sound when she stepped on it. It sounded like tinkling glass.

"And if anyone fell on it," she said to herself, "it might sound like glass breaking. That clears up one mystery. The whistling must have been the wind—and Horace ate my apple. Nothing," she added aloud, "is very much of a puzzle. Simple as A B C when you stop to figure it out. Now what on earth did Horace do with those papers?"

She had looked beside the furnace and they weren't there. They weren't anywhere around the work-bench either. And yet, judging by what Horace said, there must have been a great stack of them. Maybe he burned them before she had a chance to look them over. That would have been another mean trick, almost as bad as eating the treasured apple. She would ask him when he came home.

In the meantime, having nothing to study, she decided to work on her poster. It would be impossible to make it look worse and, with luck and the white paint, she might improve it. This was her last chance as the drawing teacher expected all posters to be turned in the following day.

CHAPTER VII

A QUEER FRIENDSHIP

FOR nearly an hour Judy worked over her painting while Blackberry frisked about, startling her now and then with noises that were unusual for a kitten. But Blackberry was an unusual kitten. His previous adventures gave testimony to that and Judy had learned not to let his playfulness annoy her. The poster was beginning to look a little better and Judy held it critically to the light.

"Anyone would recognize those bananas now," she said with a satisfied sigh. "Maybe it won't be the worst one in the contest after all."

But Judy's satisfaction was short lived. Before she left the cellar Irene Lang came in to show her poster. It was finished, painting and all.

"Why, Irene!" Judy exclaimed, "you shouldn't have bought paints. I told you to come here and use mine. But how beautifully you've done it! That child looks almost as if you could talk to her."

"I tried to make her real," the young mill worker answered. "I can't tell you how hard I tried because—because——"

"Because what?"

"Because I found out what the prize is. And how I need it!"

"Would you tell me?" Judy ventured, curious.

"I promised not to. Somebody got the information from a young man who works in the store. You'd never guess who that somebody could be."

"Then I hadn't better try. You don't seem to want me to know."

"Oh, yes I do. I'll tell you where I got the paints and then you can guess. Kay Vincent lent them to me."

"Kay Vincent!" Judy exclaimed. "Irene, the sky is falling. We must go and tell the king."

Irene giggled. "That's just how I felt about it. She's always been such a snob and then, all at once, she decides to make friends. She spent all Saturday afternoon and evening at the house and then came again yesterday. We finished our posters and then sat around the dining room table playing cards until nearly midnight.''

"Was Stephen Garry there?"

Judy suspected that he was the reason for Kay's changing attitude.

"That's the queer part of it," Irene answered. "He wasn't. Lon Edwards wasn't there either. But Dad played with us and after Kay went he said what a pleasant girl she was. He used to work for her father when he owned the furniture factory and never cared much for him."

Harry Vincent stilled owned the row of factory houses and Judy knew he had always insisted upon prompt payment of rents, making no allowance for unemployment, illness or death in the homes of his tenants.

"And Kay's just like him," she declared. "Let her be nice if she wants to, but take my word for it, Irene, she isn't making friends because she's fond of you. I'd watch her like a cat. If people we care about can't be trusted, certainly Kay Vincent can't."

"What people that we care about can't be trusted?" Irene wanted to know.

"I'm afraid Horace can't. And I care about him," Judy added a little tremulously. "I tease him and quarrel with him but I always trusted him until now. He ate an apple out of that dish of fruit." She indicated the blue bowl on the cellar window sill. "And then he didn't tell the truth. I know he ate it because I found the core."

"You can't expect people to be perfect," Irene said with a wise nod. She had plenty of opportunity to find out how imperfect they could be. This hard-working silk mill girl was no older than Judy but her responsibility made her seem older. She looked older too because she was usually tired. Her father's long illness added to her worries. A great many doctors had told him that he never could be cured. Judy's anxiety over the disappearance of an apple must seem trifling indeed to Irene.

The following evening when an opportunity came to discuss things with Horace, Judy felt glad that she had talked with Irene. She would try and see his faults through her friend's understanding eyes. But first she would ask him about those papers he had stacked up to burn. She summoned him to the cellar.

"Have you finally decided to forgive me for teasing you?" he asked anxiously.

"You mean you really ate the apple?" Judy's surprise showed him that she must have doubted it.

"No, Sis. I mean about the poster—making fun of it. It wasn't a very manly thing to do. I had a talk with Dad about it. I told him about the apple too. Gosh! It's such a little thing and yet it seems so big when you think I did it."

"But that wasn't what I called you down here for," Judy said, not answering his first question. "I had some homework to do last night and couldn't find some of my school papers. Could they have been in that stack you told me about?"

"Very likely. Did you look?"

"I couldn't find the stack of papers."

"Nonsense!" Horace exclaimed, starting toward the furnace. "They're right in plain sight. Right here—" He stopped and stared at the bare floor beside the furnace. "They were. I swear I piled them right here Sunday morning."

"What's the matter? Are they gone?" Judy's eyes grew big.

"Gone! Completely gone! If that doesn't beat anything you ever heard of! Papers don't dissolve into thin air."

"And we thought nobody came into the cellar all day long," Judy mused, thinking of the apple.

Horace stood beside her looking very solemn. He reminded his sister of the little sick boy that he used to be. Her mind traveled back to childhood days in Roulsville when she and Peter Dobbs played tag or hide and seek while Horace watched. He was older than Judy but his illness had given her a motherly feeling for him. The thought came to her now that she had been unfair.

"Honey told me to apologize for her," Judy said. "She's sorry that she left the work-bench in a mess. And I—I'm sorry that I thought you ate that apple."

"Judy! You don't think so any more?" the boy cried, his face beaming.

"I know you didn't do it," she declared. "But if we want to find out who really did do it we'll have to do some tall detecting. I have a feeling that whoever took that stack of papers ate the apple too.''

''But why? What would be their object and how did they get in when the windows and doors were locked?''

''That's where the detective work comes in. And,'' Judy added, gray eyes shining, ''I believe I have a clue.''

CHAPTER VIII

IN FLAMES

"What kind of a clue?" Horace asked eagerly. "Judy, are you sure it's a real live one?"

"Flesh and blood," she answered, "and in the form of a pretty blonde girl we both know."

"Not Honey?" Horace exclaimed. "For cat's sake, if you must suspect somebody, suspect me, not Honey!"

"I don't suspect Honey of anything, certainly not of eating that apple because it was still in the fruit dish the next morning. What I do mean," Judy went on in a hushed voice, "is that something frightened Honey—something here in the cellar. And she isn't very anxious to talk about it."

"What makes you think that?"

"Several things." Judy counted them off on her fingers as she named them. "First, because she left the work-bench so disorderly and Honey is usually neat. Second, because she said she was through with her poster. She meant *through* too because she told Lois and Lorraine today that she was not entering the contest. And third, because she acted so frightened Saturday night when Peter and I came home from the movies. It was after midnight —just the time spooky things usually happen. I asked her what was the matter and she said, 'nothing' but I could tell by the way she said it that it wasn't quite true.''

"What's your theory then? What do you think happened?"

"I don't know, Horace. I don't even think. I'll have to find out from Honey."

"But will she tell you?"

"I think she will." Judy smiled reminiscently. "I have had experience questioning Honey before. And if I just patiently draw her out——"

"Good grief! She isn't a tape measure."

"Laugh if you want to," Judy said, "but just wait and see. I'll question her tomorrow morning on the way to school, not suddenly, you know. I'll just lead up to it. And I'd like to bet something precious that I'll have the answer before we enter Farringdon Girls' High."

"You said you'd bet something precious?"

"I said I'd like to," Judy corrected him. "You know Mother objects to betting."

"We can bet without stakes," Horace said, grinning. "But I'll say this much for Honey. All the questions in the world can't make her tell something that she thinks is better untold. She wouldn't hurt anybody's feelings for the world."

"You're right there," Judy agreed. "Just the same, I'm betting that she tells me what happened in the cellar before we enter school."

The next morning Horace reminded Judy of her bet. "And remember," he cautioned her, "you said you'd find out before you entered school. So you had better allow yourself plenty of time."

"I will," she answered, looking up from her breakfast. Horace had finished his and stood holding his hat in his hand ready to start for the newspaper office. "You're early yourself," she said.

"Gosh! I've got to be early to get ahead of Donald Carter," the boy replied. "Lately he's been scooping up front page news just like he did in the old days before the Roulsville flood."

"Maybe Honey's story will be something important enough to print," Judy thought later when she was walking toward the Dobbs' apartment, "but I must be diplomatic. Something has happened to upset her dreadfully or she would never have given up painting her poster."

Judy's poster was already in the hands of her teacher. All of them were to have been turned in by Tuesday ready to be judged by experts at the department store. This day was Wednesday and so students who had not given in their drawings to the teacher would have to take them to the store themselves that morning as the contest closed at noon. The following Saturday was the opening day of the exhibit, in reality an advertising scheme to attract more buyers to Brandt's Department Store. Naturally friends and relatives of the winners would come to see the paintings. Fifty or so honorable mentions would be on display as well as first, second and third prize posters. Horace had already been assigned to interview the winners. Three students would have their pictures in the *Daily Herald*. Perhaps posters would be the best things to discuss with Honey.

Judy rang the bell to the apartment still planning her conversation.

To her surprise, Mrs. Dobbs answered and the old lady was all dressed in her black silk, a sure sign of something important about to happen.

"I had a mind to keep Gracie out of school today," she said. "We're expecting company —relatives she's never seen. I wanted her to be here to welcome them."

"But I ought to go, Grandma," Honey's voice protested from somewhere beyond the door.

It surprised Judy to see that she had just been out.

"Where were you so early in the morning?" she asked.

"Taking my morning exercise," Honey answered, trying to laugh. "There's nothing like a nice, brisk walk before breakfast to sharpen a person's appetite."

Judy, remembering Mrs. Dobbs' excellent cooking, wondered that anyone's appetite would need sharpening for it. In spite of the old lady's crippled hand she still reigned supreme in her own kitchen and often expressed grati-

tude to Dr. Bolton that she was able to work
at all. Judy had accompanied her father many
times when poor Mrs. Dobbs lay flat in bed,
crippled from a stroke of apoplexy. Now his
calls were less frequent.

Judy waited a few minutes for Honey to have
her breakfast, trying to convince Mrs. Dobbs
not to keep her out of school.

"Really, she ought not to miss her classes
and besides," she reminded her, "there's a
Civics test today."

"You're right, dearie." Mrs. Dobbs gave
Judy's arm an affectionate pat. "We mustn't
be selfish with our Honey. She belongs to her
friends and her schoolmates as well as to her
family."

"Grandma's such a dear," Honey said later
when the two girls were walking arm in arm
toward school. "I can never pay her back for
all her kindnesses."

Judy, remembering how long Grace Dobbs
had been separated from her loved ones,
thought it was the other way around.

"You're wrong, Honey," she said. "They
are the ones who are trying to pay you."

"But it shouldn't be that way," Honey ob-

jected. "I'd love to do something really fine
to make Grandma and Grandpa proud of me."

"Then why give up the poster contest?"
Judy asked.

"I didn't—not on purpose. You know we
were only given one sheet of paper. How is
yours coming along?"

"It's in," Judy answered. "Not saying how.
My opinion is that it couldn't be worse. Most
of the other girls have turned in their posters
too as they don't relish traipsing down to the
store and going through all that red tape. It
said in the paper last night that today is posi-
tively the last chance. What made you
give up?"

"Because I couldn't have any more paper."

"What happened? Did you spoil the piece
you had?"

"Not exactly." Honey sighed. "But I
couldn't use it any more. It wasn't anybody's
fault but my own. I'm so careless with things."

"It wasn't anything that happened in the
cellar then?"

"What makes you ask that?"

"Because I thought you acted frightened
Saturday night."

"But I told you nothing happened. Nothing happened to my poster Saturday night. Judy, don't you think we ought to hurry?"

"To school? Why no! It's still early and I wanted to talk."

"But everybody else is hurrying." Honey quickened her own steps as she said it and pulled Judy along with her. "There's Kay and Marge and Betty. Look! They're all running!"

"Lois and Lorraine too!" Judy exclaimed as they streaked around the corner.

It must be late to make them hurry so. But no! She could see the courthouse clock and it was only a little after eight, earlier even than she thought.

Men and boys were running too and the clang of fire engines sounded down the street. Now they were within a block of the school. The fire engines turned the corner too and shouts went up to clear the street.

"It must be near by!" Judy exclaimed, stopping a moment to get her breath. "Why, it must be—the school!"

The girls stopped, horrified. It was no use going any farther. A cloud of blue smoke enveloped the right wing of the school building and, while they watched, a tongue of flame leaped out of one of the lower windows.

Lois, Lorraine, Kay and a few other girls were standing in a group near by. Judy and Honey joined them and a general cry of, "Our posters are burning!" went up from the group. They never thought of the dreaded Civics test they were escaping. Lorraine Lee was actually in tears. Judy, too, felt a tightening at her throat, but it was not because of the loss of her poster. Farringdon Girls' High School had seemed vast and unfriendly when the Bolton family first moved from Roulsville but now every class room, every hall, every corner of the auditorium had grown dear. It was like a nightmare watching these familiar places tortured with heat.

Soon the girls were forced to move farther away from the burning school. Firemen warned them against crossing the street. Other firemen, holding the hose, kept streams of water playing over the building. In spite of this, sheets of flame crept steadily upward. Fiery tongues shot out in unexpected places and suddenly burst from the roof.

Excited cries of, "Keep back there! She's going to crash!" came to the girls' ears. They moved back with the jostling crowd. Some of them were students but a great many were just curious spectators watching for excitement.

"It's goodbye to Farringdon Girls' High School," Lois said quaveringly. "Why, it's like losing a friend."

Judy turned to Honey and met the other girl's frightened gaze without once thinking of the questions she had started to ask. Kay Vincent called out excitedly, "Come on, girls, let's sing one last song for the dear old school before the roof caves in."

CHAPTER IX

BLUE AND SCARLET

KAY was hopping all around them in her excitement. The other girls watched her, struck speechless.

"Come on," she called. "Everybody sing. It's our last chance!

"Blue and Scarlet! Blue and Scarlet!
All join in! All join in!"

Her high pitched soprano voice sounded clearly above the noise of the crowd. But not one girl sang with her.

"What's the matter?" she demanded. "Where's all that school spirit we used to talk about?"

"Oh, Kay!" Lorraine cried. "Can't you see? It's hardly appropriate—now. Everybody is staring at you."

"Let them stare," Kay retorted. "I wouldn't be making such a fool of myself if you girls would co-operate."

"And make fools of ourselves too?" Judy inquired.

Kay was about to make some unkind answer when a sound of splintering timber interrupted her. A general cry of awe went up as the roof of the schoolhouse crashed through the upper floor sending a volley of sparks skyward. Heat from the burning building could be felt against Judy's cheeks and the acrid taste of smoke was in the air. Even Kay kept silent now. Flames covered the complete structure for a moment and when they could see it again only the brick skeleton remained.

Judy, looking over the crowd, saw three boys, Horace, Peter and Arthur, standing together. Their hats were off and their heads bowed as though they were marching in a funeral procession. The thought that Horace was there to report the "big news" he had yearned for did not occur to his sister until afterwards.

"Blue and Scarlet," Honey repeated, breaking a long silence. "Blue smoke and scarlet flame. Who ever thought of our school colors taking such a meaning!"

The fire was dying now. A broken gas pipe in the basement sent up a continuous stream of fire but the woodwork inside the school changed from red coals to black embers. Water, still pouring from the hose, glistened on the sooty brick walls. Firemen had been too late to save the building itself and now bent all their efforts to keep the fire from spreading. Spacious grounds around the building helped. But, unfortunately, it was situated on the hillside. This diminished the force and quantity of water to such an extent that half the day passed before the ruins were abandoned by the firemen. Groups of students lingered longer than that to mourn their loss.

As soon as the crowd began to go home, the three boys sighted the girls and approached them solemnly.

"A tough break," Peter lamented, "darned tough! And just when you girls were all so interested in that contest. I suppose most of your posters went up in smoke."

"Mine did," Lorraine said sadly, "and I spent hours over it. If I do say it myself, it was lovely. Lois did a beautiful poster too and we both handed them in yesterday."

"So did I," Judy put in, "but as I didn't do so well on mine I won't miss it much. The colors were terrible. Now I suppose they're all black. I'll miss the dear old school."

"We all will," the others echoed.

"Didn't any of you have your posters at home?" Horace asked, consulting a pad as he spoke. Judy could see that it was filled with notations in shorthand and guessed that his paper would be grateful. Donald Carter, his rival, was nowhere in sight.

"I did," Kay Vincent answered quickly. "Why do you ask?"

"Because I have news for you. Good news for Kay and bad news for the rest of you, I'm afraid. I just interviewed Mr. Brandt, head of the store, and he says the exhibit is to be held Saturday just as if nothing had happened. There are the grade schools to be considered, he says. Also Boys' High and the Industrial High School where Irene goes."

"I'm glad for her," Judy said. "She deserves to win a prize."

"I helped her," Kay Vincent announced loud enough so all the other girls could hear. "Irene is a nice girl and I think we ought to invite her to more of our affairs. Don't you think so too, Judy?"

"I always did think so."

"Well, she and I are going down to the store this noon to hand in our posters. I saved mine out on purpose so she wouldn't feel timid going alone. We're going to the exhibit together too." Kay's confident tone of voice assured the others that she fully expected to see her own painting on the wall.

Lois and Lorraine, who were both artistically inclined, looked to each other for sympathy, then turned to Arthur.

"Can't we go home?" Lois asked plaintively. "There's nothing here any more."

"Poor little sister," Arthur sympathized as both chums clung to him. "I'll take them along," he said, turning to Judy. "But I'll be back. Maybe you hadn't heard, but all three of us fellows are on a committee to help investigate the cause of this fire."

"May I be on the committee too?" Judy asked eagerly.

"Unofficially, perhaps."

"If you don't mind searching through blackened ruins," Peter Dobbs put in, "and knowing you, Judy, I'm pretty sure you don't. And you, Honey," he added with a nod to his sister, "ought to be back home helping Grandma entertain your three great aunts. The pleasure is all yours."

"It will be a pleasure too," Honey replied. Meeting relatives was a novel experience for her. Lois took her arm and all three girls left with Arthur. Kay Vincent went too, calling back something about a date with Irene.

"Should we start investigating before Arthur gets back?" Judy asked, instantly on the alert.

"Not a bad idea," her brother agreed, "if this news is to go in the evening paper. I'll write it up with all due respect to you girls— all except Kay Vincent. I have a mind to do a little piece by itself about her solo act. It was such a ridiculous performance that it ought to make good reading."

"You heard it too?" Judy questioned. Then she lowered her voice almost to a whisper. "Did you hear what Honey said afterwards, about the school colors?"

After she told him, Horace decided to write that up too. "It's what makes a paper, the personal touch, and I won't mention any names."

"You won't need to," Peter Dobbs assured

him. "Everybody here heard Kay when she started to sing. I honestly believe some of them were afraid she was going crazy. It was the excitement, probably, and I'd go easy on her at that, Horace. She's been real decent to Irene lately and the poor kid needs it."

"There's a reason for that," Judy began. "I'd like to bet something precious——"

Horace's accusing look stopped her.

"I wouldn't say that any more, Sis."

"I said it last night," she explained to Peter. "I bet Horace that I'd find out something from Honey before we entered this school." She surveyed the ruins with misty eyes, then brushed a hand hastily across her cheek. "And—and look what happened," she finished tragically.

"What was it you wanted to find out?" Peter asked. He had taken Judy's arm to help her over the wet street. A few policemen and interested boys were already inspecting the ruined school. Judy noticed one of the officers who appeared to be very much interested in something on the rear wall. This part of the building had not fallen. Only the window frames were charred and the glass broken.

Horace, seeing a possibility for more news, went on ahead.

"I'm not interested in finding out anything right now except what those policemen are saying," Judy answered Peter's question. She pulled his coatsleeve. "Do hurry!"

CHAPTER X

Just outside the burned building another policeman stopped Judy and Peter.

"You can't go any farther," he warned them. "An investigation is going on here."

"I'm on the committee," Peter explained, "a friend of one of the *Herald* reporters."

The officer eyed him critically. "Okay, boy. But you can't take the girl with you."

"But I'm the reporter's sister," Judy objected.

"Yeah?" The policeman chuckled. "By and by his cousins and his aunts will appear on the scene. But it won't go with me. You had better both stay out."

"Is that so!" His brusque manner irritated the girl. "I suppose you're one of Chief Kelly's men? Well, I am Judy Bolton."

Her words worked like a charm.

"Not the girl who cornered Vine Thompson's gang? Excuse me, Miss. You can go ahead. Like as not you can help them in there.''

''That's my Judy girl!'' Peter's grip on her arm tightened. ''Just tell them who you are and you'll get by every time. Chief Kelly would be lost without you.''

Judy smiled in appreciation of his compliment. Coming from Peter Dobbs, the frank, straight-forward law student, it meant something. Besides, Judy knew in her heart that she had been a help to Chief Kelly and hoped that she might be able to help him again. Of all the things she enjoyed, detective work was most to her liking and, because she enjoyed it, Judy found plenty of opportunity to use her wits in that direction. Now the discovery of an open window on the first floor of the school building interested her.

''I tell you it's been forced open,'' one of the policemen said, emphasizing his statement with a thump of his nightstick on the brick wall. ''This window frame is pretty badly burned but you can still see where somebody's pried under it. The lock's torn off too.''

''You mean somebody broke into the school on purpose to set fire to it!'' Judy exclaimed.

"I'm not saying that," he replied, "but I am saying that whoever entered the building through the window caused the fire, either on purpose or by accident."

"There's news for you," Judy whispered, nudging her brother, but he was already busy making note of it.

"I hope the poor boob had time to clear out. That is," Peter added, "if the building caught fire by accident."

"If he didn't have time to clear out," the officer remarked with a grim smile, "his body will be here in the ruins."

Judy shuddered. She hadn't thought of that possibility. "And suppose the one who set the fire is still alive?" she asked.

"Well—" The officer deliberated a moment, swinging his nightstick. He had met Judy before and respected her opinions. In fact, this was the very man who had helped her back in Roulsville at the time of the flood when they seemed to be pursuing only a shadow. "Well," he repeated, "of course there's a chance that it was only a kid. But if a man entered this school and set fire to it like as not he'd spend some time behind bars."

Just at that point in the conversation Arthur returned and had to hear the story of the open window over again. Lois and Lorraine were with him. Having had a good lunch they were eager to share Judy's adventures. Judy's own lunch consisted of a hot dog sandwich and an ice cream cone, purchased at the nearest refreshment stand. Horace bought them and shortly afterwards hurried back to the *Herald* office with his story. Judy promised to telephone him right away if anything turned up.

"Not much chance of that," Arthur told the girls reassuringly. "Such fires are usually started by one of the students."

"Not in a girls' school," Lorraine objected, looking shocked.

"A girls' school or any school. What's the difference? Perhaps some student wanted a long vacation."

"I hadn't thought of that!" Lois exclaimed. "We might go away to camp or something."

"Don't, Lois," Judy protested. "Let's talk about that afterwards. Just now I'm not in the mood for a vacation. I would feel as if I were running away from something. So many mysterious things have happened lately that it seems as if some of them must have something to do with this fire.''

, ''What things, besides the open window?'' Arthur asked.

For a moment Judy leaned back against the standing portion of the schoolhouse wall without answering. Sometimes inexplicable things were better not discussed, especially when dear ones were involved.

''You never told me what you wanted to find out from Honey,'' Peter prompted her. ''Is that one of the mysterious things you're talking about?''

Girl-like, she answered his question with another question. ''Didn't you think she seemed frightened Saturday night when we came home from the movies?''

''I don't remember that she did,'' Peter replied after a moment's thought.

''Well,'' Judy went on, ''after that she gave up trying for the poster contest. And I think the contest had something to do with the fire. I don't know why I think so but I just do.''

''Maybe some girl who couldn't paint felt jealous of those who could and set the fire just for meanness,'' Lorraine suggested.

"You don't think Honey would do that!" gasped Peter.

"Of course not," all three girls cried in a chorus. Their voices implied that such a thing was unthinkable.

In spite of that Peter left them looking worried. He went to his classes at college that afternoon feeling a great responsibility for this new sister of his. Having been separated from her own family since babyhood she might have different standards of right and wrong.

Judy felt worried too. Oh, why did she have to go and suggest the poster contest as the cause of the fire? The bitter part of it was that everybody agreed with her. Now if they all blamed Honey it would be her fault. But would it? If Honey were more like her brother, Peter,—frank, honest, sincere—then no one would dare suspect her. Instead Judy feared that her old idea that lies were a "way out" still persisted. She went home late that afternoon with a sick feeling that maybe Honey did know something about the fire. The fact that she had been out early that morning, at exactly the time the fire must have started, did not make Judy feel one bit better.

The day had furnished the police with but one worth while clue—the open window. People who lived nearby had been questioned but nobody had seen anyone prowling around the school grounds. The janitor, who discovered the fire, declared that the whole lower floor was in flames and he took no time to investigate but ran to the nearest fire alarm box and sent in a call. His wife corroborated his story that he left his own house at seven forty. The fire, authorities said, must have been started before seven thirty. Judy, reviewing all this in her mind, remembered that Honey came home from her early morning walk at exactly seven thirty.

"But this time," she told herself sternly, "I'm not going to try and prove that Honey is guilty. *I'm going to try and prove that she is innocent.*"

CHAPTER XI

HORACE worked until all hours that night improving his newspaper story. The next morning he was out of the house early, still on the alert for news. Dr. Bolton, usually a sympathetic listener, was busy on what he called a case history. And when Judy attempted to discuss things with Lois and Lorraine she found that Kay Vincent had been there ahead of her.

Now Kay was often a well-behaved and nice mannered girl. It was true, she had a sharp tongue. However, most of her friends had grown accustomed to that. But Kay, angry, was a human volcano. And Kay had seen the morning paper with Horace's account of her solo act on the front page. It was written to be amusing but it had not amused Kay.

"We should have warned Horace," Lorraine wailed. "None of us stopped to consider how Kay would feel."

"Did Kay ever stop to consider how we would feel?" Judy returned pointedly. "She ought to be able to take a dose of her own medicine."

"It isn't that," Lois said, "we all know she's been mean, and will be again. Judy, she has already given out the information that you and Honey both were out of the house when the fire started. I do hope you can prove where you were."

"I was on the way to Honey's and Honey just went for a walk. What's more," Judy cried, "if Kay is going around suspecting people I'd like to know how it happens that she saved her poster when all the rest of us lost ours. And if she wasn't out of the house herself, how did she know that we were?"

"Dickie saw you and told her," Lorraine replied. Dickie Vincent was Kay's ten year old brother. "Besides," she went on convincingly, "Lois and I were both with Kay since six o'clock. We went on an early morning hike. Betty and Marge went too and we were together all the time. Kay treated us to a sumptuous breakfast in the woods."

A wistful expression crossed Judy's face, but that was only for an instant. This picnic breakfast was not the only good time she had missed because Harry Vincent's daughter objected to her presence. And, certainly, if Kay intended to accuse other people she ought to be able to clear herself of suspicion.

"But that doesn't explain why she saved out her poster," Judy said presently. "Another thing I'd like to understand is this sudden friendship with Irene. That, plus Kay's nervousness——"

"Weren't we all nervous?" Lorraine interrupted, shaming Judy with her well-controlled voice.

The next day when she went to do some shopping for her mother Judy had a chance to find out a few more things from Irene herself. She caught sight of her walking a little way ahead and hailed her. Irene might not have heard all the details of the fire and Judy felt that she must discuss it with someone—not that she hadn't been discussing it almost continually ever since it happened.

She started in telling all the details but Irene interrupted, saying that she knew them.

"You didn't see the fire, did you?" Judy asked.

"Not exactly," Irene replied with that characteristic crooked smile of hers. "But Kay Vincent met me outside the mill at noon and described it well enough so that I almost feel as if I had been there. Wasn't it lucky about Kay's poster? She would have handed it in too if it hadn't been for me. She wanted to go with me to the store and turn hers in when I did."

"And did she?" Judy questioned.

"Yes, right after lunch on Wednesday. We were just in time to enter our pictures before the contest closed. The judges were already sorting out the best pictures. I can hardly wait to see who wins. You know, the store is supposed to mail out notices to all its customers as well as to the winners. We ought to get them sometime today."

"That's a little early, isn't it?" Judy asked.

"Today's Friday," Irene reminded her, "and tomorrow is the opening day of the exhibit."

At the house Judy called goodbye to Irene and ran up on the porch. As soon as she caught sight of a letter in the mail box from Brandt's Department Store she knew it must be their announcement of prize awards.

"Irene!" she called after the retreating figure. "Irene! Come and see who won. Oh, I hope you did," she exclaimed warmly when the other girl stood beside her. "I can't think of anybody I'd rather have win than you."

"Hurry and open it," Irene cried, quivering with excitement. Her eager eyes and voice both told how she must have anticipated this moment.

"There!" Judy exclaimed, handing her the opened letter. "I'll let you have first look because your name may be there and I'm sure mine won't. My poster went up in flames and it was a good riddance at that."

Irene stood still, holding the printed notice and simply staring at it.

"Did you win?" Judy asked. "Do tell me, Irene. Or didn't you?"

What could be the matter? Judy almost wished she had looked at the notice herself. Maybe it was only an advertisement and Irene didn't understand. Then she remembered that there must be some fifty honorable mentions and perhaps she was searching for her name among them. She waited for what seemed a long time and then became impatient.

"Let me see it now," she begged. "After all, it's my letter."

"You can see it," Irene returned bitterly. "Perhaps you can understand how that awful poster of yours won first prize. I can't."

CHAPTER XII

JUDY IS DISMAYED

"First prize!" Judy cried. "Why, that's impossible. My poster burned up."

"You mean you thought it did," Irene amended.

And Judy, now holding the notice, could hardly believe her eyes. But there it was:

First Prize: Judy Bolton, Farringdon Girls' High School.
Second Prize: Irving Gray, 7B Grade.
Third Prize: Katherine Vincent, Farringdon Girls' High School.
Prize winning posters on display in the East Wing of the store from nine o'clock until five thirty Saturday, April thirtieth and every day for a week thereafter. First, second and third prize winners please call (with proper identification) and receive awards at the information desk.

Below, Irene's name appeared among the "honorable mentions." The other winners

were from grade schools, Industrial High, Boys'
High and three from kindergarten. Certainly
it did seem strange that out of all the posters
submitted first and third prize should go to
students of Farringdon Girls' High School
when only two posters from the burned school
were submitted.

"Kay told me the first prize was a wrist
watch," Irene mourned, "and I do need one.
It would help me to be on time at the mill."

"And I don't need it," Judy cried. "I don't
want it either when I didn't earn it. Oh, it's
all a mistake. My poster would never have won
a prize even if it hadn't burned up, and I have
a wrist watch."

"I haven't," Irene broke in. Her voice
sounded as if Judy were to blame.

"But it's a mistake," Judy kept saying.
"We'll clear it up somehow. Maybe the names
got mixed up or something."

She stood on the porch after Irene left trying to think of a plan but everything seemed
in a whirl. It was so unreasonable, so utterly
impossible for Judy's poster to win a prize.
How could it when it had burned up with the
school?

Presently Horace came home. He saw at once that something had upset his sister and he, too, when shown the card, simply stared at it. Then he broke the silence with an expression that he rarely used.

"Holy jumping gee willikins!"

The doctor's head popped out of his office door. "Now what!" he exclaimed.

Mrs. Bolton, too, came out on the porch to see what caused the exclamation. The announcement went the rounds and came back into Judy's own hands leaving her whole family dazed and bewildered.

"Maybe someone took it for one of these modernistic paintings," Mrs. Bolton ventured.

"Or cubistic," Horace put in, beginning to grin.

"But it was burned up in the schoolhouse," Judy cried, ignoring him. "Can't you see? Why, if that awful poster did win a prize somebody must have taken it—maybe the one who set the school on fire—and everybody will think I—I—d-d-did it." Her voice ended in a choked sob.

"Oh no, dear, they won't think that." Her mother's arm went around her in a tender embrace. "They know you too well and they like you——"

"Kay Vincent doesn't, Mother. She's already started the story that I was out of the house when the school caught fire. Besides, she's mad as a hornet about what Horace put in the paper. I can see by the way Irene acted that she's already set her against me. Oh, it's an awful mess! What *am* I going to do?"

"Do what you always have done, Judy girl," her father advised. "Use those keen wits of yours and find out what really happened. The first thing to do is call up the store and see if they can tell you who submitted that poster or when it was submitted."

"I'll do that." The detective in Judy was stirred to action and she rang the store eagerly. But it had not occurred to her that they closed at five thirty and it was nearing six o'clock when she called.

"And tomorrow," she wailed, "will be too late. That perfectly dreadful drawing will be on the wall beside all the good ones. Everybody will see how bad it is and accuse me of cheating, setting fire to the school, bribing somebody to pass it or—or——"

"Anything but murder," Horace finished for her. "Golly! If it isn't the darndest thing. What could have happened?"

"Horace!" Judy caught at his arm. "You believe in me, don't you? You're not making fun of me?"

"Of course not. I just can't understand——"

"That's what I wanted you to say—want you to say, I mean, when you write this up for the paper. Tell Mr. Lee there's been a mistake in prize awards and maybe he'll let you wait with your announcement of the winners. I know I don't want my picture in the paper. Honey was so afraid her drawing would be the worst in the class. I just wonder how she would feel to have it be the worst and still win a prize—and after it was supposed to have burned up with the school. Kay Vincent will make me miserable for the rest of my life."

Refusing her dinner, Judy went for a walk to think things out. Kay Vincent, for all her meanness, could have had nothing to do with the fire. Her presence at the early morning picnic proved that to Judy's satisfaction. The only possible clues she had pointed to Honey and there wasn't a chance of questioning her with the Dobbs apartment filled with visiting relatives.

Judy was walking down the fashionable end of Grove Street and soon realized that another course would have been better. She took a step backwards and wished she might hide in the nearest doorway. Kay Vincent was coming toward her and Betty and Marge, strong allies of Kay's, were with her.

In past experiences Judy had faced many dangers. Once she had been kidnapped. Even now she lived in a house where a woman had been murdered and rarely gave it a thought. But one thing she did fear—feared and dreaded it. And that one thing was the disapproval of her fellow students. As she once said to Peter Dobbs, she wanted people to like her.

Now Kay's voice, as she called out congratulations, rang with mockery.

"I don't deserve congratulations," Judy answered bravely. "There has been a mistake."

"Mistake is right," Kay answered, "and you're the one who made it. Even your best friends won't side in with you when they know what I know. Where were you at seven thirty?"

"Just calling for Grace Dobbs," Judy replied, trying to keep her temper. If she dared defend herself it would have been different but, to Kay's many questions she could only answer things that were obviously ridiculous. Either that or throw suspicion on Honey.

"Awfully early, wasn't it?" Kay scoffed.

"Yes," Judy admitted. "It was early but I wanted to have a talk with Honey."

"About what, may I ask?"

"You may," Judy returned, controlling her voice with an effort, "and I may answer. But then again I may not. Nobody has authorized you to question me, Kay Vincent, and until they do I'm not going to answer one more thing."

"That just proves what I told you," she remarked to the other two girls and passed on with a satisfied air of superiority that made Judy's blood boil.

"Lois and Lorraine will believe her too," she thought miserably and turned to retrace her steps. At least her family were true. But a

touch on her arm caused her to jump with surprise and there stood Arthur, a little out of
breath because he had been hurrying.

"Lois wants to talk to you," he began.

"About the poster contest?"

"I think it's that," he replied. "Anyway
I suggested that you go with us to the exhibit
tomorrow."

"Then they haven't seen the notice—or
talked with Kay Vincent?"

"Oh yes they have," he replied with a smile,
"seen and heard."

"Then you don't believe what Kay says!"

"Not if you say it isn't true."

Judy did say it. She said it a dozen times,
more or less, to Lois and Lorraine. And before
she knew what was happening the whole unpleasant matter was dismissed from the conversation and the girls were chatting gaily
about clothes.

When Judy came home she surprised her
mother by asking for something to eat.

"So the walk did make you hungry?" Mrs.
Bolton asked.

"It did more than that," Judy replied. "It

proved to me that there are people who believe in you just because you say a thing is true. And," she added, but not aloud, "that's the way I must believe in Honey. We'll solve this mystery, somehow, without accusing her."

CHAPTER XIII

AT THE EXHIBIT

Dressed in her prettiest dress, Judy tried to smile. "I'm not going to spoil Arthur's good time at the exhibit," she told Horace, "even if I do feel wretched myself. And I'm afraid my feelings now are nothing to what they will be when the other girls see my poster."

"Did Arthur say he would call for us in the car?" Horace asked. Out of consideration for his sister, he refrained from making any comments on her poster. This, he fully realized, was no time to tease. All of his boyish delight over his newspaper story vanished when he saw the trouble it was making for Judy. He could have left out that ridiculous piece about Kay Vincent if he had only known.

"Yes, Arthur is going to call for us," Judy replied with a lack of enthusiasm unusual for her. "And I expect Lois, Lorraine and Donald Carter will be with him."

"I wonder if Honey is going to the exhibit

too," Horace said presently when he and Judy were seated on the porch waiting. Arthur's car would be along any minute now.

"She and Peter will probably both go with those great-aunts who are visiting them," Judy replied. "If it weren't for that I'd like to have a talk with Honey. At least she would sympathize."

"She certainly would," Horace agreed. "That's one thing that girl is good at. I suppose all the trouble she's had herself has given her a better understanding of people. Here they come, Judy." He had seen the Pigeon turn around at the end of the park that ran through the center of Grove Street.

Judy had been the one to name Arthur's car. She called it the Pigeon because it was gray and had wings on its radiator cap. She laughed when she saw where Arthur had parked it.

"Those men who rent the garage will have a tough time getting past it if they happen along with their car just now," Horace remarked. "The trouble is, the Pigeon is so long it takes up enough parking space for two cars. Golly! Here they come backing out of the garage now!"

"Oh! I do hope they look where they are going." It occurred to Judy that they might not be able to see behind them with the shades down on the back windows.

"Watch out there!" Horace shouted. They were backing right toward Arthur's car.

"We will," Stephen Garry called back. "Congratulations, Miss Bolton! I hear you won the prize."

"Who told you? Irene?"

"Yes, and I'll be hung for a billy goat if she didn't act a bit jealous. We're on our way to the store now and may see you there."

Judy opened her mouth to tell them not to expect too much of her picture but they had started their motoi again and were edging past Arthur's car. He moved it forward to make more room.

Whenever Arthur went riding with Judy and Lorraine there was always the question of which girl should occupy the front seat. This time Lorraine's rights were undisputed and Judy climbed in the back with Lois and Donald Carter. Horace came in last and closed the door.

"You're reporting this exhibit, aren't you?"

Donald asked. "Well, take it from me, if you miss any news I intend to snap it up."

"Go ahead," Horace replied. "I've been getting the lion's share this week."

"I don't care who puts it in," Judy said, leaning back in the car with an air of submission, "but after this day is over one of you will have to write up a long explanation of why the worst poster in the class won first prize— after it was supposedly burned up. too. But don't ask me to tell you. That's something you'll have to find out for yourselves."

"If you don't find it out first." Horace modified her statement because he knew Judy well enough to be sure she would never leave all the "finding out" to others.

They were nearing Brandt's Department Store but Arthur found it necessary to park on a side street some distance away. A great many shoppers had been attracted to the exhibit. This was evidenced by the number of standing cars.

"And all of them will look at my poster and think dreadful things," Judy said as she climbed out of the Pigeon and followed the others through the maze of traffic.

Lois and Lorraine prolonged the period of waiting by shopping for feminine dainties before they went into the east wing of the store where the drawings were on display. The whole floor was crowded and, finally, Arthur suggested saving time by entering the wing through a rear door. This took them down a long aisle before they came to the walls where the posters hung. Judy could see them from a distance and kept on looking as they came nearer.

All of the drawings were beautifully done so far. But these were only the honorable mentions. The prize winners must be farther to the front where it was more crowded. As they elbowed their way through, Judy looked at first one drawing and then another, noting names of a great many boys and girls that she knew.

"Oh, there's Irene's poster!" she exclaimed, catching sight of it high on the wall. "It looks lovelier than ever. Poor Irene! And she wanted to win the prize."

"Didn't you?"

A voice at her elbow startled Judy and she looked around to see Stephen Garry standing beside her. He had kept his word and come to see her poster. He must have seen it too for he and Lon Edwards were both moving down the aisle toward the exit.

"I'm afraid mine isn't as good as these others," Judy tried to explain, "and besides I thought it burned up."

Lon Edwards joined Stephen Garry's laughter. "Don't you worry, Miss Bolton," he said. "It's hanging up toward the front and take it from us, it's swell. The judges sure knew their business when they picked you for the winner."

"Is he teasing?" Judy asked anxiously.

"Maybe." Horace shrugged his shoulders. "It takes all kinds of tastes to make up a world."

But those in the party who had not seen Judy's poster were beginning to think it might have been a good one after all. Surely it must be, they declared, to find a place with the other beautiful posters that were displayed. But Judy knew better. She almost wanted to shut her eyes and not look.

"Where is your poster?" Lois asked her "Didn't you say you copied fruit?"

"I tried to."

"But none of the prize winning posters are of fruit." She stood on tip toe and pointed. "See where they are?"

"Oh, yes," Lorraine exclaimed. "Aren't they lovely? Let's try and get a little nearer to them."

"I don't see," Judy objected. "Show me again, Lois. I don't see my poster anywhere."

Catching hold of her hand, Lois pulled her through the crowded aisle until they were standing just opposite the wall where the prize winning posters hung.

"See! It says first prize so it must be yours. Why, Judy! I never dreamed you could draw like that. I thought your poster said EAT FRUIT FOR HEALTH but this one says EXERCISE FOR HEALTH and how beautifully you printed it."

"But it isn't the printing that made it win a prize," Arthur pointed out, "it's the action she's put into those two girls playing tennis. Look at the swing to that one girl's arm! You must have copied yourself, Judy. It looks enough like you."

"I didn't copy myself."

They all looked at Judy as she spoke and saw that her face was almost colorless. Her tense voice told them at once that something was wrong.

"I didn't copy myself," she repeated. "I didn't copy anybody. Why, I never saw that poster before in my life!"

CHAPTER XIV

"You didn't!" the others all exclaimed.

"Do you mean to say," Arthur asked, "that this drawing really isn't yours, Judy?"

"It certainly isn't," she replied, still studying the picture. "Horace can tell you that it isn't and so can Irene. They both saw my own poster and I honestly did copy fruit."

"But the girl in the picture looks so much like you," Lois pointed out. "Why, it looks like all of us, just the way we play tennis on our courts. See! You can even make out the towers of our house in the background and all of the girls look familiar. Don't you think the dark haired girl you are playing with looks a little like me?"

"Why, yes," Judy admitted, growing more mystified by the minute, "and those others watching! They're Lorraine and Honey as sure as anything. See! Both of them have

107

blonde hair only Honey's is a shade darker and there are Betty and Marge and Connie Gray farther back. Someone must have been there to copy us like that. When did we play tennis last, Lois?"

"Let me see." She twirled the little package that she held in her hand and tapped it against her finger tips. "Why, it must have been before the contest started. We surely haven't played since then."

"That's right," Lorraine remembered. "It was the Saturday before Kay told us about the contest."

"How did she find out ahead of time," Judy wondered. Then she turned and began studying the other two prize winning posters. Kay's poster showed more skill in drawing than either of the other two, a skill which Judy had never realized she possessed. It must have been the coloring that kept Kay's poster from winning first prize. Its message read: EAT A HOT COOKED CEREAL BREAKFAST and showed two Dutch children, heads bowed over their simple breakfast of cereal and milk.

"Imagine Kay drawing a picture of children saying grace," Lorraine exclaimed.

She voiced the very thing that Judy was thinking. All the time, in the back of her mind, a suspicion just would crowd in that Kay was, in some way, responsible for the mistake. Could she have painted two pictures and submitted one of them as Judy's just for spite? Could she have copied the girls as they played tennis? Again Judy looked at the poster that was supposed to be hers. Yes, all the girls were there except Kay herself. Then she compared the two posters. Both of them were expertly drawn, but were they drawn by the same hand? She asked Arthur's opinion.

"I would say, no," he replied. "Decidedly no. The Dutch children are drawn merely in outline while you can see in the other—shall I say your drawing—that the artist has had to feel her way with the pencil. The tennis players took time and patience while the Dutch children took merely skill."

"You may be right," Judy agreed, still studying the two posters. Again her clues seemed to be leading her into a spider web. If Kay had done it for spite what was the game? Had she been foolish enough to think Judy would accept a prize for a poster not hers? And then had she intended to prove its rightful ownership and put her to shame?

"Come on, everybody," she beckoned the others. "Let's go down to the information desk and see if we can't find out who really submitted this poster."

The others agreed and followed her eagerly. Not one of them suggested asking for the prize although they were there to identify Judy and she could easily claim it.

"There has been a mistake," she began. "I am Judy Bolton but the prize winning poster is not mine."

She had to repeat her statement before the man at the desk understood. "I thought you might help me find its rightful owner," she added.

"We shall be glad to assist you," the man replied. "What is it you would like to know?"

"I would like to know who submitted it, sir. Could you tell me?"

He consulted a record book before he answered and studied it a few moments with knit brows.

"This seems to be one of the first posters turned in," he said at last. "We have no record of the person who submitted it, however. Usually this is done by the teacher or the student personally. I can only tell you this much, that the first prize poster was not turned in by a teacher as we received posters from the schools on Tuesday. The book shows that this one was turned in on Monday."

"Monday!" Judy exclaimed. "Why, Monday I was still working on my poster. That was the day I touched it up." She turned to her brother, eyes flashing. "Why, that was the day I apologized to you—and Honey apologized to me and Irene came in to show us her poster. Horace, do you think it would be a kindness to turn in a poster that would win a prize and put someone else's name on it? I mean, would you do it? *Did* you do it because you were sorry you teased me?"

"Why, Judy! Why, I—I—" The accusation left him speechless for a moment.

"Of course he didn't do it," Donald Carter put in. "Can't you tell by the looks of his face that he didn't do it?"

"Yes, but who would?"

That was it exactly. Who could consider such a thing a kindness? Could Honey— But

Honey couldn't draw. At least she thought she couldn't. And Irene was out of the question because she wanted the prize herself. So did Kay.

They had wandered away from the information desk and Judy, in spite of Arthur's guiding arm, kept stumbling into people. Her thoughts were becoming more confused by the minute. Oh, if there could only be some way of unravelling this mystery without suspecting —without questioning Honey.

"I could just stop in," Judy finally decided, "and mention the fact that the prize poster isn't mine. I could describe it, maybe, and see what happens.

"Arthur," she directed him when they were all in the car again. "Don't drive us right home. Drive over to the Dobbs apartment and let me off there. I want to talk to Honey."

CHAPTER XV

"THANKS, Arthur!"

Judy tripped from the car and ran up the walk to the big, modern apartment building. Mrs. Dobbs lived on the first floor and, as the outside door was unlocked, Judy went in without ringing the bell.

In the hall she could hear voices laughing and chatting—the visiting relatives perhaps. Then she remembered that it must be nearly noon and that they might be sitting at table. They would think her visit ill-timed as, indeed, it proved to be.

"Just in time for lunch," Mrs. Dobbs exclaimed when Judy finally worked up courage to ring the inside bell and she opened the door.

"Oh, I didn't mean to," the girl cried. "I just wanted to tell you about the exhibit——"

"Yes, do!" Honey ran to the door and gave her a welcoming embrace. "Tell the aunties,

113

too. I've been trying to persuade them to come this afternoon and see it. Aunt Lettie and Aunt Charlotte, this is a friend of mine, Judy Bolton, the girl that won first prize in the poster contest.''

"I—I didn't really,'' Judy protested, but the two old ladies interrupted her with exclamations of, "Splendid!'' "Congratulations, my dear,'' and Mrs. Dobbs, eyes sparkling, told them this and that about what a wonderful girl Judy was.

"Like another granddaughter to me and I'm so happy for you, my dear,'' she said, kissing Judy's cheek. "Why, I never knew you had a talent for drawing. You do *everything,* child. I never saw anything like it.''

If the old ladies noticed the blank look on Judy's face they paid no heed. They probably attributed it to embarrassment but, for ten minutes or more, they never gave her a chance to say a word without being rude and interrupting.

After that it would have sounded so queer to say, "The poster isn't mine,'' that Judy decided to wait until she and Honey were alone —if they ever were.

Mrs. Dobbs wouldn't hear of letting Judy go home without her lunch and Honey called up the doctor's house while she was still protesting.

"There! It's all fixed," she announced. "Now you'll have to stay. Your mother says so."

"I'm not hungry," Judy objected weakly.

"I've heard that before," Mrs. Dobbs laughed. "And afterwards counted the slices of cake——"

"You'll embarrass the child," Aunt Lettie put in.

"She's talking about the old days," Judy explained. "Peter and I used to play together when we were children."

The two aunts exchanged smiling glances. They considered Judy still a child, looking back over the years to their own sixteenth birthdays.

Just as they were sitting down at table Peter and his grandfather came in.

"Sorry to be late, Mother," Mr. Dobbs began and then broke off with a surprised whistle. "Well, if this isn't an honor, Judy Bolton having lunch with us again. Congratulations! I declare if some people don't get into a habit of winning prizes. We'll have a regular artist's tea with Judy present."

He came over to shake her hand and she winced from his grip. But when Peter, too, started in with congratulations she decided it was about time to draw the line.

"That's enough for now," she said in a low voice. "Peter, for goodness sake, change the conversation and don't say any more about the prize until I have had a chance to talk with you and Honey alone. Do you promise?"

"You know how I feel about promises, Judy."

"Well, don't promise then," she retorted, "but if you do say anything more I shall get right up and walk home."

"Christmas!" exclaimed Peter and sat heavily in his chair.

Judy ate. She had to eat in order not to hurt Mrs. Dobbs' feelings, but the dainty foods that were set before her tasted like sawdust and shavings. Once such a large lump came in her throat that she could hardly swallow. She reached for her glass of water and her unsteady hand upset it all over the clean cloth.

"I'll walk home with you," Peter offered after the ordeal of the meal was over and she finally had succeeded in convincing them that she must go.

"Can't Honey come instead?" she asked.

Peter eyed her quizzically. "Since when have you preferred Honey's company to mine? You're not offended because I wouldn't make a silly promise?"

"It wasn't a silly promise——"

"All right. All right," he said impatiently. "Go ahead, Honey. She'd rather walk with you, it seems."

"But I can't," Honey protested. "We were going down to the exhibit and I must stay and help Grandma get ready."

"I can walk home alone," Judy replied, concealing her disappointment with an indifferent toss of her auburn curls. She started out of the door with a curt, "goodbye and thanks for the dinner," but she had barely closed it behind her when Peter darted out and caught hold of her arm.

"Judy, what is the matter?" he asked. "You mustn't go away in a huff. Be game and let me walk along with you."

"I am game," she returned. "I guess that's all I am—just some sort of game board. Anyway somebody is having an awfully good time playing on my feelings. I wanted to talk with Honey about it. At least she would sympathize——"

"Can't I sympathize?" he interrupted gently.

"Why, yes, Peter. You can. Maybe it's better telling you after all." Her eyes sought his and found there a look of genuine concern. Oh, she hoped for his sake that Honey had not deceived them. She wanted to spare him the worry of knowing that such a possibility existed and simply told him that the first prize poster on the wall at Brandt's Department Store was not hers.

"And your aunts never gave me a minute to explain until they had me loaded down with congratulations," she continued. "Then I thought I would wait and tell Honey——"

"Why Honey?"

"Because I haven't had a minute to talk with her since the fire and I would like to find out what happened to her poster."

"She said she lost it," Peter answered, "but she didn't say where or how. I didn't ask her as she seemed so worried about it. Judy, describe this prize winning poster for me, will you?"

He had been walking along toward home with her as they talked and now they stood in front of Dr. Bolton's house.

"Come on up on the porch," Judy invited him, "and I'll tell you all about the picture—every detail."

"Okay!" He seated himself on the porch step and motioned Judy to a chair. True to her promise, she told him every detail. She described the scene on the Farringdon-Pett tennis courts and gave the names of the girls in the picture. Finally she finished up in eloquent praise of the whole poster and then turned to the abject Peter.

"Well?" she inquired.

"I can tell you who painted it," he said gravely. "Honey did."

"I was afraid so."

Judy leaned back in her chair with a sigh and the animated look faded from her eyes.

Peter continued to stare at a fixed spot somewhere beyond the porch steps.

"I'll find out why she did it," he said at last. "She couldn't have meant to cause all this trouble. Perhaps she signed your name thinking it would be a kindness to you."

"Perhaps."

For the moment nothing concerned Judy except Peter's suffering and her own. What right, she asked herself rebelliously, had this girl to cause such trouble. In spite of the disadvantages of her bringing up among strangers she must have learned the ways of honest folk. Her six months with the Dobbs family had surely done that much. Then Judy remembered Honey's tales of cruel treatment, beatings when she was a mere infant. And all that time her own family had believed her dead. The Invisible Chimes with their weird and ghostly music had helped restore Mrs. Dobbs' lost granddaughter—but all that was another story. This new mystery had nothing to do with the past. Judy could easily have forgiven Honey for past mistakes but now, with her grandparents' good example—and Peter's, there could be no excuse. She had deceived

them about not being able to draw and only
pretended that she lost her poster. She might
even have tried to sneak it into school and accidentally set the fire. . . . But Judy's mind
balked at that. Honey had no poster with her
when she returned from her walk Wednesday
morning.

"Peter!" she cried, jumping suddenly to her
feet. "Hurry home and tell Honey I must see
her. There is a chance that she isn't to blame.
If only we can get her to tell us where she
lost her poster."

Peter went, post-haste, but in a short time he
returned without his sister.

"They've gone to the exhibit," he announced. "At least, that's where I think
they've gone because the apartment is de-
serted. Come down to the store with me and
we may find them there."

"But I don't want to. It was torture enough
going down there this morning."

"Judy Bolton," he chided her. "You are
supposed to like mysteries. A regular girl
detective, I always called you. But there you
stand like a balky horse when I suggest going
ahead on this one."

"I won't be balky," she promised. "I'll be galloping right with you and if we can prove that someone else turned in Honey's poster. . . . Why, Peter, someone may have done it to be mean to her. Her poster may have been stolen. . . ."

"That's an idea!" the boy exclaimed, "an idea that's worth following up."

CHAPTER XVI

CONFESSIONS

THEY discussed the idea all the way to the store. Crowds were still going in and out— a dizzy procession surging through the revolving doors. Peter and Judy pushed their way in just as Honey and the three elderly sisters were on the way out. Laughing at the coincidence, they turned clear around with the doors and followed them.

At first Honey seemed not to notice but, finally, when she saw that Judy was almost beside her, she turned and spoke.

"Don't come home with us now," she said.

Judy started back as if she had been struck. Honey's voice was icy and tense with pent-up anger.

"Just long enough to explain—" she protested.

"You don't need to explain," Honey retorted. "I've seen the poster. I know who painted it but you may keep the prize. If you wanted it badly enough to steal my poster——"

"She didn't steal it," Peter put in, and his commanding voice momentarily silenced his sister.

"Aren't you coming?" Mrs. Dobbs and her two sisters were waiting a few paces ahead and turned and called to them.

"We'll come later," Judy called back, strangely glad. "We're going back to the store for something."

"We are not—" Honey's dark eyes were flashing. "I'll not walk a step with you, Judy Bolton. You've played the meanest, meanest trick. But you can keep the prize——"

"I haven't got the prize. It's still at the information desk. I told them there was some mistake——"

"But Judy, you didn't tell Grandma and my aunts." Honey's voice sounded at once penitent and bewildered.

"That's nothing," Peter put in. "I didn't tell them about the school fire until after I had heard all about what a fine young man I had grown to be and how much I looked like poor Uncle Tom or Great Uncle Harry—and all the time I had it on the tip of my tongue and they never gave me a minute to speak."

"You see," Judy finished, "that was it. They never gave me a minute to speak until after they had congratulated me black and blue. Then I thought it would be better to tell you alone but you wouldn't come. So I told Peter."

"Told Peter what?"

"That the poster wasn't mine and then he told me it was yours. I never dreamed you could draw like that. You didn't show me your poster."

"I wanted to surprise you," Honey confessed.

"Great!" Peter exclaimed. "Now we can go to the information desk, claim the prize and surprise everybody."

"Yes," Judy agreed. "I'd like to do that, too, but how will we explain it? What will we say?"

All three exchanged puzzled glances.

After a long silence Honey repeated blankly, "What *will* we say?"

"I can say this much," Judy declared, "and I have already said it to the man at the information desk—that I never saw the poster until this morning."

"And I can say this much," Honey went on, parroting her, "that I haven't seen the poster since I lost it in your cellar Saturday night."

"See!" Judy stopped in the middle of a crowded aisle to throw Peter a triumphant look. "I told you something frightened her."

"Wait till we're out of this jam," he answered, guiding the girls between counters, "and we'll find a quiet spot somewhere and discuss this thing seriously. We'll have to prove how the names got mixed before Honey can get her prize."

A quiet spot in Brandt's Department Store that afternoon was about as hard to find as a spring in the Sahara desert. The waiting room was jammed, but on the fifth floor in the furniture department Peter found an unoccupied sofa.

"If we lower our voices," he said with a grin, "we may be able to sit on this thing for a few minutes before some goof comes along and tries to sell it to us. Now, Honey," and his voice became serious as he moved closer to his sister, "no secrets, no surprises. Just tell us as clearly as you can remember what happened in the cellar Saturday night."

"I'll have to start before Saturday night if I tell the whole story," Honey began. "It was the Saturday before that we girls played tennis and I found out what fun it was to draw. Remember, Peter, how I sketched the girls on the back of a chocolate bar wrapper? Of course they were much smaller and Kay Vincent stood where I drew myself afterwards. Maybe it was mean but I didn't want Kay in the picture. I don't like her."

"And no wonder!" Judy exclaimed. "She had it all over that you and I were out of the house that morning the school fire started. She wanted to blame us."

"The nerve! I wish we could blame her."

It was unlike Honey to say anything as spiteful as that but Judy echoed her sentiments. She did it silently, however, and waited for Honey to go on with her story. She told how she copied the small picture and improved it until, finally, it was ready to paint.

"That took two long evenings," she continued. "Friday evening when you and Arthur went to the concert nothing happened to disturb me and I just worked away trying out colors until the picture seemed just right. I did all

the background first and only had the girls'
dresses and hair to color Saturday. That
seemed harder and I worried for fear I might
spoil it. Then I got to thinking about that
woman who was murdered in your house and
all at once I heard voices. They were like
ghosts.''

She shivered and fell silent until Judy and
Peter urged her to go on.

''I looked all around and couldn't see a soul
and still the voices sounded right next to me.
They were muffled and so low that I couldn't
hear a word. Afterwards they stopped and I
—I don't know why I did it—but I leaned my
head down on the bench and went to sleep with
the paint brush still in my hand. I don't know
how long I slept but when I woke up it all
seemed so silly that I thought I must have
dreamed it. I knew it must be late so I worked
fast with the brush for about ten minutes and
had just finished the poster when you and Peter
came home.''

''Oh!'' Judy exclaimed, ''so you really were
through with it and I thought you meant you
had given up—not finished the painting. And
you told me nothing happened because you

thought you had dreamed that about the voices?"

"Yes," Honey admitted. "That was why."

"I don't think you did dream it," Judy said, sitting forward eagerly. "Now tell us what happened to the poster."

"I can't tell you that," Honey replied, "because I don't know."

"You mean it disappeared before your eyes!" Peter exclaimed.

"Well, no." Honey's smooth, young forehead wrinkled for a moment in thought. "Not exactly before my eyes, Peter, but when I came back Monday it was gone."

"You mean you left it in the cellar?"

"Yes. It was late and I wanted to get home. I picked up the envelope in a hurry and must have forgotten to put the poster inside. I had it all finished—everything done except signing my name."

"And whoever took it must have signed my name instead of yours!" Judy exclaimed. "What a queer thing to do!"

"But you didn't say anything about it," Peter put in, more than a little bewildered by this startling revelation. "I should think you would have told Judy that you couldn't find your poster."

"I would have," Honey admitted, "but she was mad at Horace and I thought she would blame him. She said he had some papers stacked up to burn and I thought he burned my poster by mistake. I knew he would feel terribly if anyone told him about it. So I just naturally kept still."

"Good gracious!" Judy exclaimed. "You kept still so you wouldn't hurt Horace's feelings? And all the time I thought—I mean I was afraid you knew something about the fire. You were out so early that morning and I knew you weren't walking just to work up an appetite."

"I woke up with a headache. I had been crying about the poster. Sort of babyish, I guess, but I had tried so hard to make a good one. I didn't want Grandma to see my eyes red——"

"You poor kid!" Peter exclaimed, taking his sister's small hands in his own strong ones. "Gosh! If you'd only told somebody."

Judy was silent. Honey's confession revealed something that she had suspected for a long time—that Honey must like Horace and like him a lot to go through all that just to save hurting his feelings.

"And the queer part of it is," she surprised them by saying, "that Horace never burned those papers. They disappeared too!"

CHAPTER XVII

THROUGH THE MAGNIFYING GLASS

"This is what I call hitting on some real clues," Peter Dobbs declared. "You're the detective, Judy. What does it spell to you?"

"It spells a whole lot——"

She jumped suddenly to her feet. "There's a furniture salesman coming to sell us this sofa and we'd better make ourselves scarce before he scolds us for sitting on it. But one thing I am going to do," she continued talking as they stood waiting for the elevator, "is take a paper and pencil and, the minute we're home, write down all these mysterious things in the order that they happened—among them Kay Vincent's sudden friendship for Irene. She had some reason besides friendliness for saving out her poster. She couldn't have set fire to the school because she was on a picnic, but I'd like to bet something precious that she knows who did do it."

This time Horace was not there to object to her betting and Peter, although his smile told her that he recognized the expression, kept silent.

"Are you going home now?" Honey asked.

"Not right now," Judy replied. "It's almost time for the store to close but I intend to take one more good look at Kay Vincent's poster." She reached in her pocket and produced a magnifying glass that she had brought along for that very purpose. "This glass may show something that we couldn't see with the naked eye."

"Speaking of detectives," Peter said in honest admiration, "Judy, if you don't beat anything I ever heard of! Who, besides you, would think of taking a magnifying glass to an art exhibit?"

They were approaching the wall where Kay Vincent's picture hung beside Honey's. Judy paused now and then, studying them both from a distance.

"That picture is just a little too perfect for Kay to draw," she said, eyes narrowed. "And the painting is just a little too poor to go with such a fine picture. She either copied or traced it and if she traced it, this glass will soon show it. Now!"

She had taken a few steps forward and stood holding the magnifying glass over first one part and then another part of Kay's poster. Peering eagerly through the glass, she studied every line of the drawing but no evidence could she find that it had been traced.

"But there is one curious thing," she said at length. "Come here and look through this glass. What would you say made that queer smudge on the margin of the paper?"

Peter and Honey took turns and both of them saw the thing she indicated.

"It looks as if it had yeen dropped and accidentally stepped on," Peter said.

"That's just what I thought!"

Judy's gray eyes were shining as they always did whenever she became excited. And nothing excited her more than hitting upon a real clue when actual detective work was under way. It was a supremely satisfying thrill to find that her first suspicions might be well founded.

Peter Dobbs could not see why the footprint made much difference. "Anybody might have stepped on it," he told her.

"But why?" Judy cried. "If somebody stepped on it, it must have been dropped. And if it was dropped, somebody must have been frightened—and something frightened them. You see, it *is* a clue! It might mean one of two things. Either that Kay Vincent's poster was in our cellar or that it was in the burning school."

"Why? How on earth do you figure that?"

"Because somebody was frightened! And I can't think of any two places more frightening than our cellar and the burning school. You just wait and see if I'm not right."

"Betting something precious?" Peter teased her, laughingly.

"I'd like to. And now one more thing. Take a good look, Peter. What's different about Kay's poster. Do you see it?"

"I'm afraid I don't," he admitted after studying it for some time.

"I do," Honey cried, pointing. "One corner is missing. It looks as if somebody had snipped it right off with a pair of sharp scissors."

"And what's your answer to that?" Peter challenged Judy.

"I haven't any answer," she replied, smiling. "Clues aren't answers, Peter. They're possibilities. The answer will come later when we set all these things down on paper. If I can't solve this complete mystery, school fire and all, with this many clues then I'm not the detective you think I am."

"You'll solve it all right," he prophesied. "What puzzles me is how. What *do* you see in the fact that a tiny triangle of paper is missing off one corner of Kay's poster?"

"I see this. That something must have been on that corner that Kay didn't want other people to see. If we could find out what it was I'm almost sure it would help solve the mystery."

"Maybe it would," Peter agreed doubtfully. "But there isn't one chance in a million that you'll ever find that missing corner."

She laughed. "We'll hope for the millionth chance then. Come over after dinner and we will start detecting in earnest. We're going to have some fun working out this mystery together."

Judy meant what she said. She knew from experience that detective work could be fun and the poster contest had caused enough

trouble, filling her mind with doubts and suspicions. Now she knew that Horace and
Honey were as free from guilt as herself. And
Peter Dobbs . . . Judy simply couldn't imagine
ever suspecting honest Peter of anything.

That evening found an excited group
gathered in the cellar. They were armed with
paper, pencils, a ruler and a calendar. Actual
analysis on the case was about to begin.

CHAPTER XVIII

SEVEN DAYS OF MYSTERY

"Now to set down all the mysterious things that have happened since—when?"

Judy paused, pencil in air, and turned to Peter and Honey who leaned eagerly over the work-bench. Horace, too, had joined them. They intended to devote the whole evening to working out a solution to two mysteries—the school fire and who submitted Honey's poster. Although seemingly unrelated, Judy believed that if they solved the one they would find the answer to the other. Thinking back, they all agreed that mysterious things had been happening ever since Kay Vincent first announced that there would be a contest. That happened less than two weeks before—April eighteenth, to be exact. Horace drew a red circle around that date on the calendar.

"And speaking of mysterious things," Honey put in. "How *did* Kay know ahead of time?"

"That's just what I'm wondering," Judy declared and then began writing something on a slip of paper. "We'll put that down as our first clue."

"Wait a minute!" both the boys objected. "Did any other mysterious things happen that same day?"

Judy smiled with her eyes, that peculiar, knowing smile that reflected her inward joy in solving mysteries. "Did anything else happen? I'll say it did! Why, it was that very night that somebody left the light on in the cellar and I went down to turn it out."

"And then what?" Horace asked eagerly.

"Well, I stumbled over Blackberry for one thing and I'm perfectly sure that I put him out before I went to bed. And I heard somebody whistling!"

"Where?"

"In the cellar. But when I looked, the doors and windows were locked and not a soul around. Like you, Honey, I thought I just imagined it, but now I know better."

"Anything else happen that day?" Peter inquired, after an awed silence.

"Nothing very mysterious. I sent those

boarders to Irene just to help her out. That's right, they did come to our house first inquiring for rooms."

"And rented the garage and suggested putting the lumber in the cellar," Horace remembered. "We might as well put down everything, even if it hasn't anything to do with the contest."

"But that *has* something to do with the contest," Judy cried. "They built the work-bench where we painted our posters. I'll put it this way:

April eighteenth:

Kay announces poster contest. Men who rented garage offer to build work-bench. Someone left light on down cellar and let Blackberry in after I had put him out. I heard whistling.

"There! Isn't that enough for one day? Now——"

But they could think of nothing further until Wednesday when Horace fell over the pile of lumber and Judy heard breaking glass. It was hardly important enough to deserve a place on the paper, he thought, but she insisted on putting it down.

April twentieth:

Horace stumbles over lumber and we hear breaking glass. Men drive into garage with shades on the car down. They build a work-bench out of the lumber.

The next event was the concert that Judy had attended with Arthur, but she could remember nothing unusual about that. But after Saturday night when she went out with Peter Dobbs there were plenty of things to remember.

"Set down the dates," he advised her, "and "we'll all put on our thinking caps. What happened besides the voices Honey heard?"

"I forgot my poster," she reminded him. "That's all that happened to me Saturday. It was Monday that I came back and found it gone."

On paper, the facts seemed more puzzling. Before she put down anything further, Judy made a row of slanting o's while she thought. Then she erased the o's and began writing. This is what she wrote:

April twenty-third:

Honey hears voices and forgets her poster.

April twenty-fourth:
Horace cleans cellar, piles up papers and
we go out, leaving doors and windows all
locked.

April twenty-fifth:
Find someone has eaten an apple and
taken the papers on the very day Honey's
poster is turned in with my name signed on
it. Irene tells of Kay's sudden friendship.

"Now Tuesday, the twenty-sixth, what hap
pened?"

That day Judy skipped. Nothing of any importance had happened except that the girls
had turned in their posters. That was school
routine—not mystery. But Wednesday . . .

"The fire!" everybody shouted.

"And," Judy added, "the open window! I'm
going to make a note of something else too."

April twenty-seventh:
School fire. Police find window forced
open. Kay Vincent acted nervous.

"Judy," Horace reproved her after he had
read it, "why must you drag Kay into that?
Was she any more nervous than the rest of you?
And you know she was on a picnic when the fire
started."

"I wouldn't put that down either," Peter agreed.

"But I would," Judy insisted. "It may be only a woman's intuition, but I think Kay knows something about the fire."

Peter shrugged his shoulders. "I won't argue with you, Judy. You've been right too often. What next?"

"Put the exhibit down next and make it an even seven for luck," Horace suggested.

"But the announcement——"

"That had today's date on it."

"I see." Judy tapped her pencil thoughtfully on her forehead. "Well, today there are plenty of clues."

April thirtieth:
Opening day of exhibit. Find Honey's poster with my name on it, printed in neat capitals. Discover a footprint and a corner missing on Kay Vincent's poster; also find that the coloring is less perfect than the drawing.

Judy added a deliberate period and surveyed her finished work with an air of satisfaction much greater than she had felt when viewing her finished poster.

"And now," she announced dramatically, "we have the whole evening to follow up these clues."

"The whole evening!" Peter Dobbs exclaimed after he had consulted his watch. "Why, it's ten o'clock already."

"So it is! I'll tell you what," Judy went on excitedly, "I'll take them upstairs and type them on Dad's office typewriter. I'll make three carbons and give one to each of you. Then tomorrow morning come back with your solutions."

"A good idea!" they all agreed and trooped up the cellar stairs and out into the doctor's office.

Blackberry, who had been sleeping under the work-bench in a bed of shavings, got up, stretched himself and followed them.

"It's a strange thing," Judy remarked, "but Blackberry has taken a great fancy to the cellar. Every time I go down there he follows me. If cats could talk we might be saved the bother of all this figuring."

She opened the office door softly and peered in. Her father sat writing at his desk with a pile of cards from his filing cabinet before him.

"He's busy on case histories again," Judy whispered. "I'll bring the typewriter out into the living room so as not to bother him."

Peter offered to carry it and when it was placed on the table she inserted paper and carbons and the keys began their noisy clicking.

She was just typing *April thirtieth* when the door bell's insistent ringing interrupted her. Horace answered it and Judy paid little attention thinking it was one of the doctor's patients.

When the page was done she called first Honey, then Peter and then Horace to read it before she took it from the machine.

"You need a comma after 'cellar' here under *April twenty-fourth*," Horace pointed out. He reached over to show her and she caught the glint of something silver in his hand.

"What's that?" she asked, curious.

"Key to the garage," he replied. "The men just handed it to me. Said they were taking their car out tonight——"

"Are they gone?" she cried, and ran to the door to see.

"They're gone all right," Horace called after her. "What's wrong? They paid the month's rent in advance."

"But they may have known something about this mystery! Now we can't even question them and we don't know their address or anything. Oh shucks!"

She sat down at the typewriter and began typing something else under the day's date.

Men give up the garage and leave . . .

"Horace," she asked. "Did you see the car? Were the back shades still drawn? No? Then maybe they didn't take their tools with them. Maybe they never carried tools on the back seat of their car. It might have been something else!"

"But what?" the others asked.

"We may never know."

Judy sighed and the typewriter keys went on clicking as she finished her sentence:

. . . with shades up.

CHAPTER XIX

SEVEN CLUES

THE next morning, quite early, Judy sat on the porch watching through the lattice work for Peter and Honey. She and Horace had their solutions ready but had not shown them to each other. They intended to wait and compare them with the others.

As she watched, Judy saw Irene Lang going by. Her clothes were the nicest that she had ever worn and the smile that played on her lips told the girl on the porch that something pleasant was about to happen. Immediately she forgot Irene's hasty words of two days before and called out to her.

"Irene! Come up a minute, won't you?"

The other girl paid no heed but kept on walking in the opposite direction.

"Irene!" Judy called a second time. "Irene! Please come up. I want to explain something."

"I'm in a hurry. Your explanation will have to wait until another time."

"Will you come up another time?"

Irene hesitated. Judy could see that she was struggling with conflicting emotions and tried to imagine herself in Irene's place. Suppose she worked all day winding silk threads until she could close her eyes and see nothing but endless white bobbins spinning and turning on noisy machines. Suppose she came home, not to rest, but to cook food for hungry boarders. Then school in the evening and after that suppose she had painted a really fine poster. How would she feel to see the prizes go to those who had all the things she paid for so dearly. Oh, she would be hurt, jealous—perhaps even more than Irene for Judy was a sensitive creature. Friends meant much to her. Irene's friendship meant much and Judy's heart gave a leap of joy when she finally said, "yes, Judy. I'll come up another time and let you explain."

Judy sat dreaming for a while after that, the mystery almost forgotten. Her thoughts were of a group of friendly girls with no misunderstandings to spoil their confidence in each other —a group that included Irene Lang, daughter of a poor cripple, and excluded Kay Vincent although Kay's father was one of the wealthiest men in the city. They would all go to high school together, no more herding of sheep and goats. No more separating rich from poor. Irene would be just as welcome in Farringdon Girls' High——

Here Judy's thoughts broke off in a queer little moan. Day dreaming, she had forgotten for the moment that her beloved high school was a mass of blackened timbers and fallen bricks. Who could have been cruel enough . . . or careless? The dreamy look faded from Judy's eyes and in its place came an expression of determination. She studied the slip of paper in her hand. Seven clues! Seven clues that must point to but one solution.

Footsteps on the sidewalk told Judy that someone was approaching and when she looked up, Peter Dobbs greeted her.

"Well, here we are," he said, giving Honey a playful push through the gate. "Here we are all ready to begin on the double seven."

"Double what?" Judy asked, rising and coming forth from the checkered shadows of the lattice work.

"Double seven. Seven days of mystery and seven clues," he explained. "And since seven is a lucky number, fortune points in our direction.''

''So it does! But Peter, what about the solutions?''

Judy reached out an eager hand, took his paper and read:

1. Kay's advance information about the poster contest.
Solution: She may have been snooping in the teacher's desk.
2. Mysterious noises and things disappearing out of the cellar.
Solution: ?
3. Honey's poster submitted with Judy's name signed on it.
Solution: ?
4. Kay's nervousness and sudden friendship for Irene.
Solution: Unimportant.
5. Discovery of an open window in the burned school.
Solution: Tramp probably stayed there and dropped a match.
6. Discrepancies in Kay's poster.
Solution: Unimportant.
7. Men rent garage; enter with shades on car down and leave with shades up.
Solution: Decidedly unimportant.

After she put the paper down, Judy stood puzzling over something.

"It's the strangest thing," she said at length, "but your seven clues are just like mine except that I didn't think of that fancy word 'discrepancies.' I must admit, though, that I don't care much for your solutions. I disagree with you about four, six and seven being unimportant. What about your solutions, Honey?"

"I'm not much good at solving things," she admitted. "I'd rather watch you do it. Peter and I did those solutions together. I guess you and Horace didn't, though. Where is he?"

"In the house somewhere. I'll lead you to him right away."

Just as she had expected, Judy found her brother in the cellar. Blackberry, as usual, was curled in his bed underneath the workbench. Apparently he had forsaken downy cushions forever. He seemed to prefer the woody smell of shavings and the damp mystery of a cellar to the cushion where he used to sleep in Judy's bedroom. Either that or else Horace's cat, a white creature that he called Ghostie, had won the endless battle between them.

White gravel covered the cellar floor almost

completely but the faint perfume of soil lingered in spite of that. Judy attributed the "different" smell to the fact that the floor was not of cement. Lately, however, it had been more noticeable. It even occurred to Judy, as she studied her clues, that someone might have been digging. Certainly there must be some mysterious entrance to the cellar.

"And it's up to us to find it," she added with a convincing toss of her auburn locks.

"We'll start a searching party," Horace suggested, "as soon as we have compared these clues and checked up on the solutions. I figured it that there must be an entrance to the cellar too."

Peter's and Honey's joint solution as well as his own lay on the bench before him. Judy, the self-appointed director of the investigation, kept her paper and compared it with the others as she read them aloud.

"You and Peter both have the same answer for number five," she told Horace. "A tramp! Not a very clever tramp to pry open a school window when he could have slept inside the storm doors with no one to bother him. I think you're wrong about number one too. Not that

Kay wouldn't snoop into the teacher's desk if she had the chance. But you should have heard how insulted she was when I suggested that she must have found out from someone· in Industrial High. It just makes me all the more sure that she did! Knowing about the contest ahead of time gave her plenty of chance to plan all this mischief.''

''But are you sure she planned it?'' Honey asked doubtfully. No one but Judy herself had attempted to solve clue number six. The footprint on Kay's poster spelled but one thing to her—that Kay had been frightened. Therefore, she had written as her solution to the second and third clues:

Kay Vincent probably found a way to get into the cellar, took Honey's poster and entered it as mine.

''You see,'' she explained, ''this accounts for everything except the noises and they may have had a perfectly natural cause. Most spooky things do. The wind may have done the whistling, though it didn't sound much like it, and the gravel on the floor does crackle a little like breaking glass. The voices may have been people talking just outside, perhaps the men who rented the garage.''

"It did sound something like their voices,'' Honey admitted, ''except that it had such a hollow sound.''

"Maybe that was what frightened Kay Vincent and made her drop the poster,'' Judy cried. "She naturally would be frightened entering someone else's house and taking things.''

"She naturally would be,'' Peter put in, "*if* she did it. I, for one, don't believe that there is a secret entrance to the cellar. You would have been robbed of more valuable things than old papers.''

Horace and Honey were inclined to agree with Peter but Judy remained staunch in her belief that Kay Vincent was at the bottom of the mischief. Her friendship for Irene strengthened that conviction. Now if she could only get Irene to talk.

A few minutes later when Mrs. Bolton called them upstairs and invited the visitors to stay for dinner, Judy caught sight of Irene coming up the street. She ran out on the porch and called her.

"Remember your promise? Do come up. I want Honey to see your new dress."

"Oh! This?" Irene glanced down at the dainty gown as though realizing, for the first time, that she was wearing it. "I must go home and change it, Judy. Really, I must, before I spoil it."

Judy laughed. "I'll ask Mother to put an extra large napkin on the table for you. Peter and Honey are staying for dinner and we want you to stay too."

Irene looked up with a faint smile and it was then that Judy noticed the odd expression to her face. She could tell that something had happened, but not the pleasant something that Irene must have been expecting when she started off earlier in the morning.

"Do come," she pleaded. "I want to more than explain. I want you to help us solve something—a mystery, Irene. After dinner I'll lend you an old dress of mine while we all go exploring."

CHAPTER XX

"I HADN'T planned this kind of a time," Irene said later when Judy was helping her into one of her own serviceable dresses. "But Dad didn't expect me home for dinner. Now I won't need to explain. He—he hates to see me hurt."

"I do too." Judy put an arm about Irene's slim shoulders and gave her an impulsive hug. "I wouldn't have had that happen about the poster for the world. You must have felt terribly blue about it."

"I did. But it's almost impossible to be mad at you, Judy, when you're always doing such surprising things. I went home the other day telling myself that I would never speak to you again—and here I am not only speaking but even letting you lend me a dress. I notice you're not wearing the wrist watch."

"It's still at the store." Judy smiled, glad that Irene had mentioned it. Now it would be

easier to tell her about the mistake. Irene sat
on the edge of the bed surprised into silence
as she listened to the whole story, beginning
with the day Kay first announced the poster
contest.

"And we must solve the mystery of how
Honey's poster came to be entered or I'm
afraid they won't give her the prize," Judy
finished. She showed Irene the typewritten
page containing all the suspicious notations
about Kay Vincent and watched her face as she
read it. She fully expected Irene to take Kay's
part.

Presently Irene looked up with a peculiar
smile. "So you think there's a secret entrance
to your cellar and Kay came in here and stole
Honey's poster? What possible reason could
she have for doing such a thing?"

"Just to be mean," Judy replied. "Kay
often does things just to be mean."

Knowing of the new friendship between Kay
and Irene, Judy expected a quick retort. It
surprised her that Irene made no answer but
stood looking thoughtfully out of the bedroom
window.

"Let's go downstairs where the others are,"

she said at length. "I don't believe Kay came near this house but, just to show you I'm not mad, I'll try and help you. Ask all the questions you please about Kay and the boarders too. I'll answer them."

"Good girl!" Judy exclaimed.

She and Irene joined the others in the living room and Judy announced, much to their surprise, that she intended to go over all the clues once more before they started exploring the cellar.

"Irene may have something to tell us," she said, smiling mysteriously, "and I'm going to question her in the presence of you three witnesses."

"Awfully legal," Peter chuckled. "I hope I do as well when I'm through with law school."

Joking about the matter seemed to have taken Irene's thoughts from whatever was troubling her before and she did not become serious again until Judy asked her first searching question.

"What do you know about Kay's poster?"

"I watched her paint it," Irene said after a pause. "Really, I never thought it would win a prize. She didn't mix her paints as carefully as I did. I suppose it was because she drew it so well.''

"Did you see her draw it?"

"No," Irene admitted, "but she painted it at our house on Sunday afternoon and I sat at the table opposite her. So you see, Judy, she couldn't have had anything to do with taking Honey's poster if it disappeared Sunday. She didn't go home until almost midnight and then all three of us walked home with her.''

"You and the two boarders?" Judy questioned.

"Yes. She seemed quite interested in them. I wouldn't be surprised if you were right, Judy, and she made friends with me because she wanted to 'make' Stephen Garry. You're right about something else too.''

"What?"

"That Kay Vincent is mean. I think she's just about the meanest girl that ever lived.''

"Why, Irene!" Honey exclaimed after a shocked silence. "I thought you and she were friends.''

"I thought so too—until today." Irene glanced at the pretty pumps and sheer stockings that she wore. "I bought these," she explained, "and that dress upstairs on purpose to wear to a party at her father's bungalow. You know, Mr. Vincent has a summer place on River Road and they're just opening it today. Kay invited me to go down there with them. She said Betty and Marge and Connie Gray and a lot of other girls you know were going too. She told me to call for her at ten o'clock this morning and I could ride with them in the car. You know I don't go to parties often. I haven't been to one since that Ghost Party you had on Halloween, Judy. I did look forward to it so. And I bought the dress. It cost a lot too," she added, "more than I could afford. I had it charged at Brandt's thinking I could pay for it with the board money but now that the boarders are gone it will take weeks of saving to pay for it out of what I earn at the mill. And I suppose Kay's father will be just as mean as ever about the rent."

"Meaner, perhaps." Judy already anticipated the ending of Irene's story. She had heard of Kay's methods of dropping people when their friendship was no longer useful to her. Just as she expected, there hadn't been any party and Kay had gone on to the bungalow with her mother. The maid who answered the door bell, Irene said, told her that much and her manner implied that Irene would not have been welcome even if there had been a party.

The story brought forth exclamations of disgust from both the boys.

"Gosh, Judy," Peter exclaimed. "You may be right after all. Kay Vincent may have had a part in this poster business. A girl that would play a trick like that would do anything. I don't wonder that you think she stole Honey's poster and was responsible for the school fire."

"But she couldn't have been," Irene objected. "I'd like to blame her too after what happened today, but how can I? She couldn't be at our house and at your house both at the same time. And she couldn't have started the fire because she was on a picnic. None of the girls got back until after the school was in flames."

"That's what you call a perfect alibi," Peter remarked. "Now to break it down."

"You can't do it," Horace declared. Ever since his unfortunate story appeared in the

Daily Herald Judy noticed her brother's reluctance to criticize Kay Vincent. She guessed it was more his natural timidity than any friendship for Kay. Honey, lately, agreed with Horace no matter what he said, but it was plain that Peter would soon be thinking Judy's way.

She had been watching Irene and wondering —wondering so many times that she found it hard to decide what question to ask next. Among other things she had been wondering about Irene's boarders.

"Why did they leave so suddenly?" she asked.

"They said the work was done." Irene sat forward in her chair and the sudden animated look in her face told Judy she was about to relate something of importance. "What puzzles me," she went on, "is the kind of work they were doing. I overheard something they said once and it sounded as if they were in some illegal business. One thing I did find out is that Lon Edwards' father used to be the saloon keeper. They lived here in Farringdon a long time ago and later moved to Canada."

"And I thought they were so nice," Judy sighed.

"Well," Peter put in, "perhaps they are. Boys aren't responsible for what their parents do."

Horace, who had been thinking in his usual queer way, jumped up from his chair. His hair stood out in every direction.

"You might as well burn up all those clues about Kay Vincent," he cried excitedly. "You were right about the boarders, Judy. What a sap I was to let them get away! For all we know those birds were members of Vine Thompson's old gang, just snooping around the house as an excuse to get away with more hidden jewels. We may have overlooked a few places."

"Chief Kelly searched the house," Judy put in. But she, too, shared the excitement. "They may have been in the house somewhere whistling and breaking glass and taking stacks of old newspapers. But it sounds silly, doesn't it?"

"It does at that," Peter agreed.

"But if we find a secret entrance to the cellar—" Judy broke off, glanced at the others and then started toward the cellar door. "What geese we are!" she exclaimed. "Here we sit talking when we could be doing something. We could be exploring the cellar! I have the magnifying glass and Horace, get a chisel or something sharp. I intend to go over every inch of the wall looking for a secret door."

CHAPTER XXI

THE SEARCH BEGINS

"THIS is the most exciting thing we ever did!" Irene exclaimed as she followed the others to the cellar.

Irene Lang had helped Judy and her friends hunt for clues before. When the attic was supposedly haunted she stood, terrified, watching Judy and Horace climb up there through an opening in the ceiling. She had attended Judy's ghost party too and knew the strange history of the large, rambling house with eye-like windows where the Bolton family lived.

Mysterious things were always happening because Vine Thompson, fence for her gang of robbers, went to every extreme concealing stolen goods. Judy and Horace had found jewels, money and many other things hidden in the house. Now it was beginning to look as if some new revelation was about to be made.

The only thing about it that disappointed

Judy was the fact that she had felt so sure Kay Vincent had a part in the disappearance of Honey's poster and now all evidence seemed to be pointing toward Irene's boarders. Horace summed it up beautifully.

"You said, Judy, that mysterious things began happening the day Kay Vincent gave out the announcement about the poster contest. Well, I say they began happening the day those two Canadians rented our garage and they kept on happening until they left last night. I was in the cellar all morning and didn't hear one freakish thing."

"I guess you're right," Judy agreed. "When Irene's boarders leave all the mysterious things go too. It is queer, though, why Kay Vincent took such an interest in them."

"They were young and good-looking," Honey put in. "Why shouldn't she take an interest in them?"

"I suppose she should," Judy replied, still looking dubious. She didn't want to be wrong about Kay Vincent. It would make her appear catty to the other girls. Already she was beginning to wish that she had said less to Lois and Lorraine for they were friends of Kay's.

At the foot of the cellar stairs. Irene paused, looking frightened.

"It—it smells funny down here," she said.

"What of it?" Horace asked. "It's probably the dampness. It isn't an unpleasant smell."

"I should say not," Peter agreed.

Still Irene hesitated. "I'm afraid," she said in a shaky voice. "The mill girls are always saying things about this house. They all believe in spirits. And those voices you heard, Honey! I think I would simply die if anything spooky happened."

"What could?"

"Anything," Irene replied. "Vine Thompson was murdered here."

Brave as they were, none of the searching party spoke for a moment after that. None of them believed in spirits. They had disproved Irene's superstitious theories time and again. Still there was that apprehensive silence. They might be wrong and she might be right. Things had disappeared. Voices had been heard.

"Judy," Horace directed her. "For cat's sake, turn on that light."

"It is on," she answered. "It doesn't shine much. Or maybe it just seems dark. Irene, why must you scare us just when we're all prepared to enjoy this searching party?"

"Go ahead. Enjoy it," she said. "I merely stated a fact. It was nothing new. You all knew the robbers shot her. Maybe you didn't know, though, that she was murdered right in this cellar."

Judy hadn't known. The story of Vine Thompson and her gang of robbers had unfolded itself, bit by bit, ever since the Boltons moved into the house. That was the previous Fall. Interest had centered in the attic at first, then in one of the bedrooms. But all the mysterious happenings had been explained. No need to be frightened. Judy's mind told her that. But something else, over which she had no control, held her motionless. The strange odor that permeated the air seemed more stifling than sweet.

"What about this chisel?" Peter inquired shortly. "Want me to start hunting in this corner?"

"I wish you would," Judy said, relieved. "I'll begin with the magnifying glass. It really is light down here. Funny that it seemed so dark for a moment.''

''You're not nervous, Judy?'' Peter teased her. Then he began tapping on the wall with the chisel, prying to see if any stones were loose. Judy went ahead of him peering through the glass, ready to tell him the instant she saw anything strange. The others, although supposed to be members of the searching party, simply stood still and watched. Judy noticed that Horace had an arm about each of the two girls. She giggled and nudged Peter.

''See that! And I'll bet he's as scared as they are. But there's nothing unusual down here now.''

''No?'' he glanced quizzically at the slim figure beside him and chuckled. ''What about this queer smell?''

''What about it?'' she asked. ''I'm sure I don't know what it is.''

''I'm glad you don't,'' he replied. ''But in the old days of Edwards' corner saloon it must have been a bit more familiar.''

''You mean it's whiskey!''

He nodded.

''Irene! Horace! Honey!'' Judy called

out. "Peter thinks this smell in the cellar is whiskey! But who would bring anything like that into our cellar?"

Forgetting that they had been afraid, the three came forward eagerly.

"You're not solving the mystery," Honey scolded her brother. "You're just getting in deeper and deeper. I don't believe there is any secret entrance because you have already searched over half the wall."

"There's *something*," Judy declared. "And we'll go over the whole wall and the ceiling and floor too if necessary. But we'll find out what it is. See if we don't! Why don't you take that ruler you're holding, Horace, and help?"

After that all was quiet except for a continual tapping against the stone wall. Horace followed Judy's suggestion, going in the opposite direction from Peter. Both Irene and Honey tried to help him but they had nothing but bobbie pins to work with.

The scratching noise of the pins caused Blackberry to come suddenly forth from his bed underneath the work-bench. Like a black flash, he sprang at the side of the wall. Honey gave a start and Irene screamed.

"It's only Blackberry," Judy chided them. "If we keep close watch of him he may show us something. He knows how he got in after I put him out. Now if he would only go out the same way."

"We might scare him," Horace suggested.

"You will not. That would be cruel. But I do think it would be a good plan to go outside and call him. I'll do it," Judy decided and ran up the cellar stairs.

Soon they heard her voice outside calling the kitten and Honey observed that it sounded not at all like the voices she had heard.

"I could tell in a minute that was Judy," she said, "but those other voices sounded— sounded—well, I can't say where they sounded but they didn't sound outside."

"Watch Blackberry!" Irene cried.

All eyes turned eagerly toward the cat. He was going in circles and sniffing the gravel on the floor.

Presently Judy came back and they told her what had happened. The cat was now sitting on his haunches looking reproachfully at his mistress. It was not like Judy to call him unless she had something for him to eat.

"He knows you cheated him," Horace said, "but why do you suppose he sniffed the gravel instead of going upstairs and yowling at the door?"

"There's just one reason," Judy declared. "And if I am right we are about to make a startling discovery. Horace, you go upstairs and get the broom and see if you can't find a couple of rakes or hoes for the rest of us. We're going to remove every trace of gravel from this cellar floor and find out what's under it."

"Ugh!" shivered Honey who had been much impressed by the murder story, "suppose we find Vine Thompson's bones."

"Or her spirit," Irene added in an awed whisper.

"It'll be her spirit all right," Peter Dobbs chuckled. "From what I've heard, most of her spirit came out of a whiskey bottle and if my nose knows, she kept her liquor somewhere in this cellar."

"But we're not looking for liquor," Honey said plaintively. "We're trying to find out what happened to my poster and who entered it in the contest and signed Judy's name. I really do want the wrist watch—ever so much.''

"I did too," Irene began and then closed her lips. There was no reason for Irene to be jealous of Grace Dobbs' success. She had heard her strange story from Judy and knew that Honey's life had held as little luxury, up until just lately, as had her own.

Just then Horace returned with two brooms, a rake and a battered snow shovel. He distributed these all around, giving a suitable implement to each member of the group. Then he found a coal shovel for himself.

"Now Blackberry," he told the cat, "smell your hardest and show us whereabouts this mysterious cat hole is."

The cat eyed him with typical feline dignity and then started washing himself as unconcerned as if nothing out of the ordinary had ever happened in the cellar.

"Not much help do we get out of him," Horace grunted.

"Begin shoveling there where he's sitting," suggested Judy.

She lifted the cat and moved him a safe distance away from the place where they were to begin.

Soon the gravel rattled into a pile as all of them worked industriously. At first nothing but packed earth showed underneath. Then something else rattled and Blackberry made a dive for it.

There, half hidden by the white gravel, was part of a strong, iron chain. A ring at the end of it showed Judy that it must be attached to something. It must be meant to pull.

"Stand back, everybody!" she cried. "Peter, you're strong. Get hold of that chain and the rest of us will help you. All ready?"

They had formed in a line behind Peter, each holding the other's waist. Irene and Honey were at the end, watching in wide-eyed amazement. Judy stood just behind the two boys. As she gave the signal they all pulled.

At the same time a crashing of gravel was heard, accompanied by a loud bang. Something certainly had happened, and happened so suddenly that Honey and Irene were both knocked off their feet.

Too excited to think of helping them up, Judy and the boys rushed forward and stood for a moment gazing at something so strange that it left them speechless. The chain had been attached to a trap door in the floor of the cellar. Now the door yawned wide and below it Judy could see the dim shape of a ladder leading down into the blackness below.

"Horace!" she called out to her brother. "Give me that flashlight out of your pocket. I'm going down this ladder!"

CHAPTER XXII

"COME on down," Judy called presently. "It's the oddest place you ever saw."

Honey's face went white. Judy's voice had the same hollow sound that had frightened her before when she heard voices in the cellar.

"We ought to go down," she said shakily to the others. "Something might happen to Judy."

"I couldn't climb down the ladder," Irene objected. "I'd get scared and fall."

"Is there room for us all?" Peter shouted into the open trap door.

"Plenty," came back Judy's muffled voice. "You've got to come down, every one of you. I think I've found the solution to the whole mystery. At least, Horace, I can explain the breaking glass."

Her brother was first to descend the ladder and the others followed as quickly as they dared. Irene hesitated, said something about tearing her new stockings, but her curiosity would not let her stay behind. She followed last of all and soon the five explorers stood on the dirt floor of a second cellar. Judy's flashlight shed its weird glow on the wall and with it flickered a moving white shadow.

A gasp was heard, and then a nervous laugh.

"It is spirits," Irene declared. She was shaking like a leaf and her face looked ghostly in the dim light. "Those voices you heard, Honey—ghosts—" Her voice trailed off suggestively and Honey finished the sentence.

"Or men—maybe robbers. They were right here for this is where their voices sounded."

"But that white thing . . ."

"It's the reflection from a broken bottle," Judy explained "See!"

She played the flashlight over a section of the wall and the circle of light revealed a row of empty shelves, empty except for one broken bottle. Here the odor that Peter noticed in the upper cellar was so strong that there could be no mistaking it.

"More of old Vine's crooked work," Horace muttered. "It looks as if she did some bootlegging on the side."

"And," Judy added impressively. "The liquor must have been stored here until last week when Irene's boarders took it away."

"My boarders!" gasped Irene. "How could they?"

"That's where the secret entrance comes in. I can tell from the direction of this tunnel just about where it ends. But first we're going to follow it and see if I'm right."

Judy led the others and continued talking as she searched with the flashlight. "See, it goes this way. The boarders must have let Blackberry in through the other entrance and that is how I happened to find him in the upper cellar after I put him out."

"It seems queer," Horace reflected, "to have an upper cellar and a lower cellar. All kinds of ghastly things may have happened in this tunnel. What's that?"

The others turned as he said it and when they saw what had frightened Horace he looked a little sheepish. Blackberry was climbing down the ladder. But the cat certainly made an eerie picture as his agile body descended noiselessly. It cast a long shadow that looked almost like something alive creeping down the wall of earth behind him. Irene shivered and clutched Horace's arm.

"There's something about cats that I don't quite like," she said.

"Nonsense!" he exclaimed. "They're all right when you get used to them. I was half planning to give you Ghostie. He and Blackberry don't get along together."

Completely forgetting her unusual surroundings, Irene cried out in delight, "Oh, I'd love to have him. I do like cats after all, only," she added, "not black ones in cellars."

"Peter gave me Blackberry," Judy said thoughtfully, "and he and I have been friends ever since."

The cat was being quite a help just then. He padded along ahead of the searchers until he came to what looked like the end of the tunnel. There he stood and yowled.

"Now what does that mean?" Peter asked. With his shoulders stooped and his head lowered, he was following close behind the cat. Judy still held the flashlight. She carried the magnifying glass in her other hand and looked the part of a professional sleuth. Suddenly she stopped, bent and picked up a wrinkled bit of paper and, with a startled cry, called the others to see what she had found.

"It's one of my missing test papers," she exclaimed. Then she held the magnifying glass over it and pointed out the curious twists in the paper.

"Now smell it," she went on excitedly. "Just see for yourself if it hasn't been wrapped around the bottles that Irene's boarders must have carried away. That proves something else, too. It proves what happened to that whole stack of papers, including Honey's poster."

This startling discovery left the others speechless for a moment. Her mind had been quicker than theirs to take in the situation and it surprised Horace that she should be so sure.

"Aren't you jumping at conclusions?" he broke the silence by saying. "First you blame Kay Vincent for everything and now you turn right around and blame Irene's boarders."

Judy smiled at him. "Maybe I am jumping at conclusions. But just you wait and see where this tunnel ends. I think I know already."

"If it ends in the garage," Peter put in,

"then you have solved the mystery all right. But you were wrong about Kay Vincent and Honey's poster. One of Irene's boarders probably turned it in after they saw they had taken it by mistake."

"That's what I'm afraid of," Judy admitted, still studying the crumpled bit of paper. "I remember now that I told them Dad said I had a talent. He must have meant a talent for solving mysteries but they thought it was a talent for drawing and the poster was mine. As it had no name signed on it, they printed my name and turned it in. Oh, I see it all now! I don't care if they are crooks and were sneaking in here to steal old Vine's booze, that, at least, was pretty decent of them."

"I—I liked them both," Irene faltered. "And I felt sure from what they said that they were working for pay."

"This kind of pay!" Peter displayed the label from the broken whiskey bottle that Judy had found. It was dated, nineteen thirteen. "Old as the hills and twice as strong," he added, wrinkling his nose.

"Watch out for your head!" Horace warned him. But the warning came too late. Peter's head, as he stood up, hit the top of the tunnel with a loud bump and a volley of small stones rattled down. At the same time a curious grating sound could be heard. A ray of light streaked suddenly across his face.

"Holy Mackerel!" he exclaimed. "The tunnel's caving in on us!"

Panic seized Irene and Honey. They stumbled blindly toward the ladder, tripped over the cat and, with mingled cries and yowls, all went down in a heap. Horace, a little less frightened than they were, tried to help them.

In the meantime Judy and Peter had made a discovery. The tunnel had not caved in but the streak of sunlight came through another trap door at that end. Here, at last, was the secret entrance. This trap door, like the one in the cellar, must have been concealed by scattered gravel as all the small stones that hailed down from overhead were round and white. With a thrill of expectation, Judy remembered that the garage, too, had a gravel floor.

"Get the ladder!" she shouted. "Horace! Help Peter carry that ladder. I want you boys to put it up to *this* trap door."

Honey stood up and rubbed her eyes as if she had just wakened from a peculiar dream. Irene, big eyed, huddled close to her and watched. Soon the two boys came back through the tunnel carrying the ladder between them.

There were many shouted directions, combined with the noise of falling gravel. Peter and Horace were pushing with all their might but the trap door opened slowly. Dust and rattling stones kept anybody from seeing, for a moment, and then the door swung open and the space was clear. The noise of wood scraping against the side of the opening told Judy that the ladder was fixed in position. Peter started up but one rung cracked under his weight and she decided it would be better for one of the girls to go first.

"You, Irene. You're the lightest."

"Mercy no!" the frightened girl exclaimed. "I'd never dare. There's no telling where this tunnel leads to."

"It can't lead very far away from the house," Judy said, "and the beams that show overhead look surprisingly like those in the roof of our garage."

After a little pause, she started climbing up

the ladder herself.   Then she turned to her brother and smiled wickedly.   "I may jump at conclusions but, if you will take notice, they are usually right."

"You were wrong about Kay Vincent," he retorted.

"I'm not so sure about that," Irene spoke up quietly.   "Now I do remember something strange that happened Sunday afternoon."

CHAPTER XXIII

NIPPED IN THE BUD

"HERE we are," announced Peter Dobbs as soon as all of the searchers were standing above ground once again. Now there could be no doubt about the tunnel. It went from the cellar to the garage—cleverly convenient for the transportation of illegal and ill-gotten liquor.

"Here we are," he repeated and seated himself on the running board of the doctor's car. "It looks, Judy, as if your father would have to be mighty careful about renting the vacant half of this garage. How about reserving it for me?"

"Fine, Peter, when you get your car. But just now I want to hear Irene's story. What happened Sunday to make you think that I was right about Kay Vincent?" Judy asked.

Irene looked about apprehensively. "This garage gives me the creeps. Come out on the porch, everybody, and we will discuss it like ladies and gentlemen. But first can't I wash and put on my good dress?''

Judy smiled at her indulgently, as though she were a child. Poor Irene, enjoying her ''good dress'' in spite of the fact that she must skimp and save to pay for it. ''Go ahead!'' she told her. ''We could stand some cleaning up ourselves.''

Within a short time the group of five were reassembled on the porch and, to look at them, no one would suspect that they had recently emerged from a tunnel underground.

Irene pointed and they all peered through the lattice, eager to hear her explanation.

''You see our front room window,'' she said. ''Well, that is right where Kay sat practically all day Sunday. I noticed that she kept looking out and once I looked too and saw the boarders driving out of your garage——''

''With the shades on their car down,'' Judy anticipated. ''And they must have been carrying out the liquor.''

''That's what I think,'' Irene continued, ''and Kay must have known what they were doing. Let me take those seven clues a minute, Judy.''

She handed them to her and Irene read them.

"I know where Kay got her advance information," she said suddenly. "They announced the poster contest at our school and I told Stephen Garry. He must have passed the information on to Kay."

"Exactly," Judy agreed, smiling her satisfaction. It was beginning to look as if Harry Vincent knew all about the crooked work that went on within the walls of the haunted house. "He may have even known about the secret cellar and told Irene's boarders."

"Or they may have told him."

Irene reversed the order of the sentence because she distinctly recalled the boarders speaking of "that old pinch penny" and the description fitted Mr. Vincent perfectly.

"That was it then," Judy decided. "Lon Edwards' father may have delivered the booze long ago and just lately told the boy about it. Then, in order to make a little money, he and Stephen Garry cart it away."

"But where?" Peter questioned. "They weren't gone long enough to take it to Canada and they left with their shades up. I was wrong," he admitted, "when I marked that seventh clue 'decidedly unimportant.' It looks now as if it is about the most important of them all.''

Judy sat studying a leaf that curled itself inside the lattice work. She began picking it to pieces, just as, in her mind, she was tearing to pieces Kay Vincent's perfect alibi. All at once she stood up.

''I know what happened to the liquor,'' she announced, her voice ringing with excitement. ''I'd like to bet something precious that Harry Vincent hired those two boys to cart it into his own cellar and stationed Kay at Irene's house as a sort of look-out. He doesn't get all his money from rents, believe me! He probably sells plenty of booze and gets fancy prices for it. I'm going to tip off Chief Kelly and have him issue a search warrant. I'd like to have Harry Vincent arrested for unlawful entry, too, but the big sneak knew we would be suspicious if he rented the garage. So, instead, he hires a couple of boys.''

''And tried to cheat them out of their pay,'' Irene added, sharing Judy's excitement. ''I'm sure that's what they meant when they said they'd get caught themselves if they tried to sue him. They've learned their lesson, I bet."

"Yes, and we'll teach Harry Vincent his," Judy cried, her eyes flashing.

Chief Kelly, the next day, was greatly interested in Judy's story. But what chiefly concerned him was the fact that the policemen who searched the house right after the murder had overlooked the trap doors.

"Two of 'em, at that!" he exclaimed, tapping his pipe thoughtfully against the edge of his desk.

Judy stood beside the desk watching him. She had grown very fond of the brusque chief of police. The many suspicious doings connected with the Bolton house brought her into frequent contact with him. He seemed to take her story more seriously, even, than she expected.

"Harry Vincent must have known all about Vine Thompson's crooked business," he ruminated, "and since the house belonged to him, he likely shared in the profits. I've been suspecting his connection with a roadhouse out River Road way for some time. The queer part of it," and here the chief began to chuckle as if it gave him a good deal of pleasure to tell it, "is that Harry Vincent is running for mayor of

this city. We'll nip his political ambitions right
in the bud if this story gets out, Miss Judy.''

"It will get out all right," she returned,
laughing. "My brother still reports for the
Daily Herald."

Before she left the police station Judy had
obtained from Chief Kelly a written statement
that would prove Honey's right to the poster
prize. She planned to meet Honey in the waiting room of Brandt's Department Store at
noon.

When Judy arrived she found the whole
Dobbs family waiting, even the visiting great-
aunts. It was easy to forgive Peter and
Honey's absence all day Sunday, they declared.
What young people wouldn't be interested in
secret doors and underground tunnels?

Honey took them to the wall where the prize
poster was on display and Judy held the magnifying glass against it so that they could see
how perfect it was in every detail. The
magnifying glass showed something else too, a
portion of Honey's poster that had been
wrinkled and ironed out again.

"That's proof of what I told you," Judy declared. "And it's no wonder Irene's boarders

were so interested when they heard I won the prize. They even came down here to see the poster.''

''Do you suppose,'' Peter asked suddenly, ''that they may have tried to sneak the poster back into the school building and accidentally set it on fire?''

''Oh, no,'' Judy replied. ''The man at the information desk said the poster was turned in Monday. That school fire is one mystery we've failed to solve.''

''It looks that way,'' Peter agreed. He stood for a moment puzzling over something and then turned to his sister. ''How about it, Honey, what say we collect the prize?''

She agreed and her eyes were dancing as she presented Chief Kelly's written explanation at the information desk. The clerk studied it critically.

''Sorry to disappoint you, Miss Dobbs,'' he said, ''but we are withholding the prizes until next Saturday. On the closing day of the exhibit they will be presented formally to the winners.''

''Does that mean with a little speech?'' Honey asked.

The man laughed. "Speech and entertain-ment. Our judges feel that a few mistakes have been made and the posters must be studied more carefully. There's no doubt about the first prize going to you, though. Over on the bulletin board it tells all about it."

He indicated the wall space next to the elevators and Honey, eager to learn more, went with her family and all of them read the bulletin carefully.

Judy walked a little behind them, thinking. Did the judges, too, suspect that Kay Vincent's poster had been copied? Could it have made a difference to them that one corner had been snipped off with scissors?

CHAPTER XXIV

IRENE'S BIG CHANCE

THAT evening Judy danced up on the porch of Irene's shabby little house. She was bubbling over with excitement.

"Irene!" she called, "they told me down at the store that a few mistakes have been made in the prize awards and if we're right about Kay copying her poster you may win a prize after all."

"Really!"

"Yes, and I know what third prize is—a five dollar credit slip at the store. Each of the honorable mentions get a dollar credit. Did you know that?"

"No, I didn't. How did you find out?"

"It's on a bulletin down at the store," Judy answered. "They tacked it up just before we left. There is going to be a fancy entertainment too, next Saturday morning when the prizes are given out. You must wear that pretty new dress and come."

"With you?"

"Of course," Judy answered. "And with Lois and Lorraine and Honey and the boys. You're one of us now."

Irene puzzled over that, not knowing what to say.

"I'm supposed to work Saturday," she said finally. "I really mustn't take a day off. We can't afford it. And I can't afford to go around with your crowd either," she added mournfully. "I would rather stay home than go places looking shabby. The dollar credit really isn't very much when I already owe the store for a dress."

"They don't pay you much in the mill, do they?" Judy asked after a pause.

"Not what I earn," Irene replied bitterly.

"In a doctor's office they would."

"What do you mean, Judy?"

"I mean this," she replied. "Dad has been so busy lately that I hardly even see him. He said today that if he could get a girl to take care of his files and answer the telephone he'd pay her twice what you're earning. He said he wanted somebody capable and conscientious and dependable. You're all of those things, Irene. Why don't you apply?"

"But I don't know anything about medicine."

"You don't need to know anything except what Dad tells you. I help him lots of times."

Irene was silent for a moment. Suddenly she threw her arms about Judy's neck and she felt a hot tear against her cheek.

"That would be—wonderful!" Irene exclaimed. "Now I won't need the wrist watch. I won't ever need to go to that terrible, noisy mill again. You didn't know, Judy, but all the girls there aren't as nice as the ones you know and it's hard to close your ears to some of the things they say."

"I didn't know," Judy answered, "but I could guess. Come home with me now and let's tell Dad who his new office girl is."

Irene ran for her hat, eager and bright-eyed. All the way to the doctor's house she was asking question after question. Would she need to wear a white uniform. Would she receive all of the doctor's patients. Would she be allowed to assist with minor operations at the doctor's office. Judy had seldom seen her so happy.

On the porch, they met Horace. He sat reading the paper and stroking the white cat which curled contentedly on his knee. It was Ghostie and Irene reminded him of his promise to give her the cat.

"But I may decide to keep it here after all," she went on delightedly and then told him about the new position she hoped to fill.

"Congratulations!" Horace gave her a warm handshake. "I'm congratulating you now because it's a sure thing. Dad couldn't find a better girl than you are. But just now he's out making a call and you'll have to wait. Here, sit with me and look over the latest revelation in print."

He offered her a chair and a page from the *Daily Herald* where, in a conspicuous place, the story of Sunday's discovery appeared. In another column was an account of the resulting raid on Harry Vincent's roadhouse where quantities of liquor were found stored.

"Pretty good write-up, eh?"

"Wonderful! And did you do it, Horace?" Irene inquired. She sat with her eyes glued to the spot in the paper where her own name appeared in print.

"I did it," he replied. "And how! Harry Vincent's chances of being mayor after this are about as fat as a match."

"It's funny how a man like that gets the nerve to run for office," Judy reflected. She was seated on the porch step at Irene's feet, her chin cupped in her hands.

"I suppose," she went on thoughtfully, "that there are plenty of people who will be scandalized to see their angelic Mr. Vincent crash down from his pedestal."

"Speaking of angels," Horace put in dramatically. "Here comes Harry Vincent in miniature."

He pointed to the street where Dickie Vincent marched along, hands in pockets and head in the air.

"He's on his way to our house and to the other houses in the row," Irene exclaimed. "He's coming to collect rents. Dad's home alone and I don't want the little nuisance bothering him. I'll have to call him up here and explain."

"I'll explain him," Horace muttered. "Why doesn't the old man come himself?"

"Dick dares to say words he wouldn't use. It might hurt his campaign."

"Dick!" Irene called out. "Don't go to our house. Dad's alone."

"Gimme the rent money and I won't," the boy retorted.

"I'll give you part of it if you'll come up," Irene conceded. "But I'm afraid you'll have to wait for the rest. I don't get paid until next Saturday."

"You got to give me all of it."

"Here, young man," Horace broke in. "You'll take what you get and no fuss about it either. Make sure he gives you a receipt, Irene. I don't like this idea of sending kids out collecting rents."

"I can't give her no receipt, smarty," the impudent little fellow sang back at Horace. "The receipt's made out for the whole business and my dad signed it. He says 'get that rent or tell 'em out they go.' "

"But it was only due yesterday," Irene gasped. "I'm paying you half of it too, if you'll only give me a receipt. I don't intend to pay it twice."

"I tell you I haven't got no receipt for half the rent."

"You must have a piece of paper in your pocket, or something you can write on," Judy put in.

The boy grinned. "See anything you can write on?" he asked as he pulled a stringy mass of match sticks, fish hooks, lines and crumpled gum wrappers out of his pocket.

Judy eyed the heap with interest. "You *might* put it on a gum wrapper or the back of a chocolate bar wrapper." She turned to Irene. "You didn't know that Honey sketched that prize winning poster of hers on the back of a chocolate bar wrapper, did you?"

Irene shook her head and looked surprised while Dick still stood there rummaging through his pockets. Finally a triangular piece of paper fell out. At first Judy thought it looked clean enough to use for a receipt.

"Why not write on this?" she asked and stooped to pick it up from the step where it had fallen. Dick stooped at the same time and their heads came into rather violent contact.

"Excuse me," Judy hastened to say.

"Excuse nothing," the boy muttered "Where's that piece of paper?"

"In my hand. We were going to use it for a receipt."

"We were not. Gimme it. Gimme it!" he shouted again when she did not answer.

But Judy stood right where she was, **mo**-tionless, holding the triangular bit of paper.

"Why do you want it?" she demanded. She looked directly at Dickie Vincent with her searching gray eyes and the little fellow suddenly hung his head.

"Leave the rent go till Saturday if you want to," he said to Irene in his meekest tone. "I'll tell Dad you couldn't pay it." He turned and was about to go away but Judy caught hold of his shoulders and whirled him around so suddenly that he stood for a moment dazed.

"You had better stay here," she warned him. "There's something I want you to explain to us. What is that little triangle of paper? Where did you get it and how did it happen to be burned along the edges?"

CHAPTER XXV

JUDY'S TALENT

DICKIE VINCENT'S arrogance left him. Instead he was sullen, refusing to answer Judy's question.

"Well, if you won't tell me, I'll tell you," she said finally. "That corner of paper is off your sister Kay's poster, isn't it? And you sneaked into the schoolhouse to get it——"

"I did not," the boy retorted. "I went in to get Kay's magazine."

For a moment Judy felt tempted to shout her triumph. She hadn't been sure about the triangle of singed paper. Her instinct for solving riddles told her that it might be so and she had accused Dickie Vincent on a wild chance. Now, by his own confession, she knew he had been inside the burning school. Another thing Judy knew and that was if she wanted the rest of his story she would have to extract it from him in the same manner. She couldn't let him know his confession had surprised her. So she continued questioning him in a well-controlled, even voice.

"Oh, the magazine that Kay used when she copied her poster?"

"She told me to get it," the boy defended himself. "She left it on top of her desk right where the teachers might see it."

"And you got her poster too, just in case the teachers had discovered that she copied the picture?"

"She didn't copy it exactly. It was a Cream of Wheat advertisement and she left off the box of cereal and when she colored it she put on different colors."

"And it was a little dark in the school and you lit a match and accidentally dropped it among Kay's papers——"

"Say, what is this?" Dick snapped. "A cross-examination? How'd you get all this dope?"

Then Judy laughed. She just couldn't help it. "I got it from you, Dickie Vincent . . . and thanks! I'll keep the triangle of paper."

All this time Horace and Irene stood staring at Judy. It was not until after Dick had broken away and started, as if he were pursued, for home that either of them spoke.

"He forgot the rent!" Irene exclaimed.

"And no wonder. Wait till I tell Dad this," Horace cried. "Speaking of talents. Sherlock Holmes himself couldn't have beat that one. And when I report the prize winners . . . Wow! Won't Kay Vincent's story be a hot potato!"

"We'll have to tell them down at the store and I shouldn't wonder if Chief Kelly has a few more questions to ask Dick Vincent when I get through telling him what he told me. And I was only guessing," Judy added with a laugh.

"Your guesses are better than some people's arguments. Mine, for instance." This was Horace's admission that he had been wrong about Kay Vincent. It came with difficulty as the boy delighted in showing off his superior knowledge. But he was always ready to acknowledge defeat and the newspaper story that his brain was busy planning crowded all other thoughts into the background.

At the store the following day Judy met Arthur and his sister. It was a relief to be able to tell Lois that Kay really had cheated and copied her poster from a magazine advertisement. Judy knew that some of Lois' crowd thought her accusation of the Vincent girl unfair.

When she had completed her revelation about the fire, Lois and Arthur added to the evidence against Dick.

"Remember," Lois said, "how he noticed you and Honey out of the house. He was just trying to blame you to get out of trouble himself. And I do believe Kay planned that early morning picnic on purpose for an alibi. It wasn't at all a usual thing to do."

"Kay is more to blame than Dickie," Arthur put in. "She is older and had no right to put her little brother up to such mischief. No wonder she was nervous about the fire! Shall we go with you, Judy, when you give out this latest bit of information?"

"I'd love to have you," she exclaimed. "You'll strengthen it."

After the story was told to the judges Judy enjoyed an ice cream soda with Arthur and Lois at the store's tea room and then went to the east wing where the posters were on display. Judy, as usual, carried the magnifying glass. She found it a more useful article than her mirror and compact and kept it in her pocketbook.

When she looked for Kay Vincent's poster, however, she found it gone. She had intended to show Lois and Arthur how Dick's footprint on the paper made her suspicious. She had been right about the person who dropped that poster being frightened. Who wouldn't be frightened, dropping a match in a desk full of books and papers? Also she intended to fit the corner on the poster as proof that it had been near the fire.

Now she forgot all these things and a little sound of delight escaped her lips. She had seen what poster took the place of Kay's and wanted to be first to tell Irene.

"We'll excuse you then," Lois said, smiling, "but don't forget, now that the mystery of the school fire is solved, we must start planning our long vacation. I know of a dear little camp up in the Thousand Islands and we want you to go up there for a couple of weeks with us. I'd like to get together a whole crowd of girls. So ask as many of your friends as you like. There's no chance of the camp being overcrowded in May."

"You're a dear!" Judy cried. "I'm sure Dad and Mother will let me go. And wouldn't it be nice if Irene and Honey could go to the Thousand Islands too?"

"Yes, and Betty and Marge and Connie, but not Kay," Lois added. "Irene can take her place in our group. Now that she's working for your father she may be able to attend Girls' High School with us."

"Why, Lois, Girls' High School is burned to the ground."

"I know it," she replied, smiling. "Didn't it ever occur to you that it might be rebuilt?"

"Oh, of course. But it will be months and months before we can go back."

"Are you sure?" Arthur asked. "I'm bidding for the contract to build it——"

"The new high school!" Judy interrupted excitedly. "Oh, Arthur! Wouldn't that be wonderful! Be sure and plan a swimming pool and a big auditorium."

"I will," he assured her, "*if* I get the contract."

"There's no such a word as 'if' with you," she called over her shoulder as she turned to leave.

Lois had a little shopping to do but Judy couldn't wait. She was so anxious to tell Irene that the third prize was really hers and not Kay Vincent's at all.

She found Irene in her father's office busy with the files and smiling over them. She looked up when Judy opened the door.

"Well, how do you like it?" she asked.

"I *love* it," Irene replied. "Your father is a perfect peach. We've been doing case histories together and it's simply fascinating. It makes me feel closer to my father too, understanding his sickness. Harry Vincent was his boss when the paint poisoned him and we've found a witness to testify that the men never had proper instructions about using it. We may be able to collect something for all these years Dad couldn't work."

"You certainly ought to!" Judy exclaimed. "It would serve Harry Vincent just right if you collected *all* of his money. He never earned a cent of it. But I guess he's just about through pulling the wool over people's eyes. Maybe Peter has learned enough about law to give you some good advice when you bring suit against him and we both know my dad will help. He thinks your father may get well pretty soon.''

"He told me. Oh, Judy! I can't tell you how happy I am.''

"Do you think anything could make you happier?''

"I don't know." Irene leaned back in her chair and sighed ecstatically. "It would have to be something wonderful to make me any happier than I am right now.''

"It is something wonderful. You are the winner of the third prize award. They took Kay's poster down this morning and put yours up in its place. Lois said you could take her place in our group too. She wants you to come with the rest of us for a vacation in the Thousand Islands and go to Girls' High when the new school is done.''

"And all because of what you found out!" Irene cried. "Oh, Judy! Honey and I may be the prize winners but you . . . you are the prize!''

"I'll say she is!''

Peter Dobbs' head popped through the door. He had been just in time to hear the last of Irene's sentence but it was no puzzle to him.

Honey had just been talking with Lois and heard all about Judy's marvelous solution from her.

"And we came to help you celebrate, you and Irene too if she can get away."

This was Honey speaking outside the office door. She danced inside and stood smiling beside her brother.

"There's a surprise out there," Peter said. "And Irene must come if it's only for half an hour. I want to take you both riding in my new car."

"Oh, Peter, and you'll keep it in our garage?"

His eyes twinkled. "Yes, Judy, if you're not afraid I'll sneak in through the tunnel and take that something precious that you're always betting."

The car was indeed a surprise. Peter had no name for it but it was a cozy affair that looked like a roadster. The difference was that when you opened the door you discovered room for five instead of two.

Honey and Irene climbed into the back seat and Horace arrived just in time to keep them company. The seat of honor, next to Peter, went to Judy.

"We'll be celebrating all summer in this," she declared as she tossed back her pretty auburn curls and smiled at the passing scenery.

She was thinking of Thousand Island Camp and the many adventures ahead of her during her long vacation. She did not yet know that "The Ghost Parade" would provide even more thrills than she anticipated. But she loved adventure and thus the world seemed to smile at her as the car sped on.

THE END

THE NANCY DREW MYSTERY STORIES

by Carolyn Keene

Here is a thrilling series of mystery stories for girls. Nancy Drew, ingenious, alert, is the daughter of a famous criminal lawyer and she herself is deeply interested in his mystery cases. Her interest involves her often in some very dangerous and exciting situations.

THE SECRET OF THE OLD CLOCK
THE HIDDEN STAIRCASE
THE BUNGALOW MYSTERY
THE MYSTERY AT LILAC INN
THE SECRET AT SHADOW RANCH
THE SECRET OF RED GATE FARM
THE CLUE IN THE DIARY
NANCY'S MYSTERIOUS LETTER
THE SIGN OF THE TWISTED CANDLES
THE PASSWORD TO LARKSPUR LANE
THE CLUE IN THE BROKEN LOCKET
THE MESSAGE IN THE HOLLOW OAK
THE MYSTERY OF THE IVORY CHARM
THE WHISPERING STATUE
THE HAUNTED BRIDGE
CLUE OF THE TAPPING HEELS
THE MYSTERY OF THE BRASS
    BOUND TRUNK
THE MYSTERY AT THE MOSS
    COVERED MANSION

GROSSET & DUNLAP

Publishers

NEW YORK